"I am Captain Jonathan Archer of the Starship Enterprise . . .

. . . I represent the people of the planet Earth."

Archer waited now for the Fazi Draa to speak. Hoshi had warned him a number of times to only speak in the same length of sentences and on the same topics as the councilman addressed. But what those topics might be, Hoshi had had no idea.

"This is an historic day," Councilman Draa said, "for the Fazi people."

"It is also an historic day for the people of Earth," Archer said. He felt constrained by this structure. He wanted to talk with them, not parrot their words.

But he didn't want to scare them either. Maybe, over time, they'd get used to human impulsiveness.

After Archer spoke, Councilman Draa sat down. The silence in the large council chamber seemed to grow with every second. Archer had no idea what he was supposed to do next.

ENTERPRISE™
BY THE BOOK

Dean Wesley Smith & Kristine Kathryn Rusch

Based upon STAR TREK®
created by Gene Roddenberry
and ENTERPRISE™
created by Rick Berman & Brannon Braga

POCKET BOOKS

New York   London   Toronto   Sydney   Singapore

This book is a work of fiction. Names, characters, places and incidents are products of the author's imagination or are used fictitiously. Any resemblance to actual events or locales or persons, living or dead, is entirely coincidental.

An *Original* Publication of POCKET BOOKS

POCKET BOOKS, a division of Simon & Schuster, Inc.
1230 Avenue of the Americas, New York, NY 10020

Copyright © 2002 by Paramount Pictures. All Rights Reserved.

STAR TREK is a Registered Trademark of Paramount Pictures.

This book is published by Pocket Books, a division of Simon & Schuster, Inc., under exclusive license from Paramount Pictures.

ISBN: 0-7434-4871-5

First Pocket Books printing January 2002

10 9 8 7 6 5 4 3 2 1

POCKET and colophon are registered trademarks of Simon & Schuster, Inc.

For information regarding special discounts for bulk purchases, please contact Simon & Schuster Special Sales at 1-800-456-6798 or business@simonandschuster.com

Printed in the U.S.A.

For Kevin

in memoriam for his favorite RPG character, Seymour.
[Kev, does this mean I can finally
stop apologizing for killing him? KKR]

ONE

"MARTIANS AREN'T GREEN," ENSIGN HOSHI SATO SAID, her delicate features twisted into a frown. "Actually, there is no life on Mars except a human colony."

The mess hall of the *Enterprise* fell silent, only the background drumming of the engines keeping it from feeling completely tomblike. The room was slightly cold, the faint smell of dinner hung in the air, and outside the windows the now familiar streaking of the stars during warp drive painted a picture of a ship in smooth flight.

Everything was going well except in here.

Ensign Elizabeth Cutler sighed and looked at the other two players. They were watching her expectantly. Ensign Travis Mayweather crossed his arms and leaned back in his chair, his expressive chocolate brown eyes filled with amusement. Crewman James Anderson, looking frail next to Mayweather, leaned forward as if the fate of the galaxy rested on Cutler's answer.

Cutler shook her head in amazement and stared

down at her notes. She'd spent a week's worth of her off-duty hours designing this science-fiction role-playing game, trying to come up with good scenarios—and trying to remember the rules. None of the other three crew members had ever played an RPG before, but they wanted to give it a try if she acted as game master. And like a fool, she had agreed.

When she was a kid, Cutler and her friends had played role-playing games, one right after another, their computers linked into a network of make-believe, eating up hours, days, entire weekends with the flights of adventure and fantasy. But now she was dealing with three adults who had only heard of RPGs—and with only her memory for help. The ship's computers just couldn't be used for this kind of recreational activity.

So she had worked out details of a science-fiction role-playing game. She had even gone so far as to convince Chief Engineer Charles "Trip" Tucker to give her a small cupful of square-shaped, very short bolts. Since there were no dice on board, she had to come up with something to let the players of her game move their characters and make decisions. She had painted the bolts red on one side, white on the other. Red was always positive. White meant nothing.

But with all her preparation, she had never expected to run into players who just couldn't seem to let their minds make things up. And that was critical to a role-playing game. Everything that went on in a game happened in the mind and through the imagination. She was going to have to get that across quickly, or this entire idea was going to be a giant bust.

"For this game," Cutler said, looking up into the attractive face of Hoshi, then glancing at Ensign Travis Mayweather, "Martians are green. And little, and have big ears and very sharp teeth."

"Can't we call them something else?" Hoshi asked. "Perhaps they came to Mars on a transport or—"

"We said we were playing a twentieth-century RPG," Anderson said. He raised his pale blond eyebrows as if for emphasis. "They believed in Martians, right, Elizabeth?"

"Right," she said, grateful for his interruption. Cutler liked Anderson. He was one of the smartest and most imaginative of the younger members of the crew. He had bright green eyes and brownish hair and a smile that could charm paint off a bulkhead. Like her, Anderson was stationed in the science department. His specialty was geology, while hers was exobiology.

"Now," she said, "let's pretend here. The Martians are like no alien race we have run into. Okay? They are the first bad guys you're going to have to deal with."

Hoshi still looked confused, but Mayweather and Anderson were nodding.

"What exactly is our goal in this game?" Mayweather asked. He gave Hoshi a sidelong glance. She ignored him.

Cutler couldn't think of two more different players. Hoshi was the ship's language expert and she'd already shown herself to be a mixture of brilliance and timidity. Mayweather had experience in deep space already, because he had grown up with his parents on cargo ships flying slowly between outposts. He seemed to love adventure, but sometimes his desire for new experiences made him seem impulsive.

"Your main goal," Cutler said, "is to keep your character alive through all the adventures."

"That's a good idea." Mayweather's eyes twinkled.

"If you're really successful and you like the game, then we can use these characters in a future game, months down the road."

"Months?" Hoshi said.

"We wanted something that would take a long time," Anderson reminded her.

"I was thinking of a game that would spread out over a few nights, not a few months."

"Nights, months." Anderson shrugged. "Out here, we got all the time in the world."

"Universe," Mayweather corrected.

"Universe," Hoshi repeated, and closed her eyes.

It was well known that she hadn't wanted to come on this trip, and rumor had it that she'd asked Captain Archer to find someone to replace her when the first mission ended. He had refused. She was trying to get accustomed to the trip, but she still seemed nervous.

Cutler was of the private opinion that some people were cut out for space travel and others weren't. Cutler knew she was; she suspected Hoshi wasn't. That was why she'd been surprised when Hoshi had volunteered for the game.

"Your second goal," Culter said, "is to collect enough parts of a Universal Translator as to be able to build it."

"A complete Universal Translator will never be possible," Hoshi said, her frown deepening.

Cutler bit back a retort. She'd decided on a Universal Translator as the goal because she'd known Hoshi was playing. Cutler thought it might make the game more interesting for the ensign.

But Cutler should have known better. Hoshi Sato was one of Earth's top linguists, personally brought on board by Captain Archer himself. And she had already helped them through a number of tough situations with alien languages. So if anyone knew if a perfect translator was ever going to happen, it was Hoshi. But being right or wrong about a translator at this point didn't matter.

"This is just a game," Cutler said, smiling at Hoshi. "Remember, we're making all this stuff up. A group of humans and aliens—your characters—were taken to Mars for this mission. All this is make-believe. Okay?"

"It has to be," Mayweather said, "since we'd only gotten to the moon in that century."

"And Mars doesn't have little green aliens," Hoshi said. "Or a translator."

Cutler sighed. "Exactly. Nothing is real in this game. Okay? Just let your imaginations roam all you want. That's the fun of this."

None of them were smiling. Not a good sign, as far as Cutler was concerned. This might turn out to be the shortest role-playing game in history.

"So," Anderson said, "what are the rules?"

Cutler glanced down at the notes about the game that she had worked out from memory and logic over the last few days. With luck she had most of what they were going to need. Some things she figured she would just have to make up as they went along.

"Well, first we need to figure out each of your characters. Anderson, pick a name for your character."

"We only get one?" Anderson asked.

Cutler resisted the urge to shake her head again. "Believe me, one will be plenty."

"Okay," he said. "My character's name is Mr. Doom."

"Mr. Doom?" Mayweather asked. "What about Dr. Doom?"

"Been done," Anderson said. "It's *Mr.* Doom."

"Human and male?" Cutler asked, smiling at the great character name.

Anderson nodded. "You got it. Very male."

She picked up the cup of bolts, shook it, and handed it to Anderson. "Roll the bolts to determine your character's strength."

He took the cup and dumped it on the table between them. The clatter of the bolts hitting the hard surface echoed in the empty mess, as if some machine had just fallen apart. Luckily, they had the room to themselves at the moment. Cutler would have to find a cloth pad to dump the bolts on for the next session. That sound was so loud, it was no wonder Captain Archer didn't hear it on the bridge.

"Five red," Cutler said, counting the red-up bolts. "That means your character, on a scale of one to ten, has a five strength quotient."

"What good are they?" Mayweather asked.

"Your character runs into a situation, just like in real life, you have to have abilities and tools to use to solve the situation." Cutler looked at three frowning faces. She waved a hand in dismissal of their questions. "I'll show you how it factors in when we get to the first situation. Anderson, roll the bolts again."

Again the noise of the bolts clattering on the tabletop filled the mess hall.

"Five intelligence factor," Cutler said.

"Your guy is sort of average," Mayweather said, "for someone with the name *Mr.* Doom."

"Mr. Mundane," Hoshi said. "You should change the name."

Anderson just glowered as the others laughed. For the first time Cutler felt this might have a chance. She led Anderson through his next few rolls, giving his character charisma (another five), dexterity (a four), and luck (another five). She had decided to leave out all the skills relating to magic, since this game was science fiction, and that shortened the character rolling time considerably.

"You'll all start with zero experience points," she said, "but you'll acquire them as the game goes on."

"I get how strength, dexterity, luck, and intelligence help," Anderson said, "but I'm not getting the charisma and the experience."

"I'll say," Mayweather said with a smile.

Anderson gave him another glower.

"Charisma determines leadership," Cutler said. "If your five is the highest charisma roll, you lead the group."

"Fighting force, led by the evil *Mr.* Doom," Mayweather said in a theatrical voice.

"The evil, mediocre Mr. Doom," Hoshi added.

"You haven't rolled yet," Anderson said ominously. "What about experience?"

"I would think that's obvious," Cutler said. "The more experience you have, the better choices you'll make."

"Let's hope," Hoshi said, and somehow Cutler thought she wasn't talking about the game. But she let the comment slide.

Cutler made Mayweather go next and he came up with an alien named Unk. After two loud rolls, Unk came up weak with only three bolts, but smart with eight bolts. He had a charisma of seven—"Sorry, Doom," he said to Anderson—a dexterity of five, and a luck of seven.

"I don't like how this is shaping up," Anderson said.

"We can't all be equal," Mayweather said.

"I remember something about being created equal," Anderson mumbled.

"Not in an RPG," Cutler said, unperturbed. They were getting interested now. She only hoped she could hold Hoshi.

Hoshi called her human woman Bertha, which broke them all up. Hoshi would not explain her reasons for the name, no matter how much the others pushed. She rolled a strength level for Bertha of eight bolts and an intelligence of four. Her charisma score was ten, her dexterity an eight, and her luck was nine.

"Well, this is a crew," Mayweather said. "A weak but smart alien, an average guy, and a strong but not too bright woman. Sounds like the perfect away team to me."

"Except the dumb one will lead us," Anderson said.

"Hey!" Hoshi said. "That's not fair. I don't want to lead."

"Then order someone else to do it," Cutler said. "You've got the charisma."

"Great," Hoshi muttered.

Still, she seemed interested. Cutler could sense the excitement at the table. No one had looked out the windows in the last fifteen minutes—and the crew was still new enough to look out the windows all the time.

"You people ready to tackle Mars?" Cutler asked.

"You have the place we are going all made up?" Anderson asked.

"I do," Cutler said, not wanting to admit she had only the first part of the adventure worked out. She had wanted to see if anyone was interested in trying it before she spent any more time on it.

"Well, let's try this then," Mayweather said.

Cutler nodded, took a deep breath, and then with a glance at her notes, started to outline what the three were facing.

"You've landed on the side of a massive red sand dune, not more than a hundred paces from the banks of the grand canal."

Hoshi said "There aren't canals on—" before she stopped herself and smiled. "Sorry. I'll get into this. I promise."

Cutler smiled too, but continued. "The canal runs beside an ancient Martian city, now in ruins. You have been informed that there might be part of the illusive Universal Translator buried in a vault in the center building of the city. Your job is to find it and return to your ship. You have six hours of daylight to cross the canal, get into the city, and find the part."

Cutler looked at her three players. The men looked back at her. Hoshi was actually taking notes.

"Now remember," Cutler said, going on, "this is a dangerous place. You have been told that there are large serpents in the canals and that the green Martians who live in the ruins of the city love to attack humans and aliens."

"Are we going in there unarmed?" Mayweather asked.

"Sounds like a suicide mission to me," Anderson said.

Cutler pressed the heel of her hand against her forehead. "I knew I was forgetting something."

She consulted her notes on weapons. "Listen up," she said. "I'm not letting you look at this."

Mayweather and Anderson searched for their own padds. Hoshi waited, poised and ready.

"I had no idea this was going to be like school," Mayweather said under his breath to Anderson.

"We never fought green Martians in my school," Anderson said, then set his padd on the table. Mayweather placed his beside Anderson's.

When they were ready, Cutler read them the weapons information. They dutifully wrote it down.

"Each of you will start off this mission with these weapons," she said. "When these weapons are used up or destroyed, you can't get more without returning to the ship. Understood?"

All of them nodded while reading.

Cutler pushed on, feeling as if she had almost got

them to the point where they actually might like role-playing. "I ask you questions about what you want to do. You can ask me questions about the settings. When you take an action, I will tell you if there is a consequence to the action or not. Then we'll roll the bolts to see how you do. Okay?"

"Roll the bolts," Anderson said, trying the phrase.

"Like rollin' dem bones," Hoshi said.

"What's that?" Mayweather asked.

"It's a slang term that came from—"

"Ready to start?" Cutler interrupted on purpose. She knew from experience that sidetracks could prolong a game. She'd seen it on the nets when she played as a kid. "So what do you want to do first?"

"Okay, we're standing in front of the canal," Anderson said, obviously checking.

Cutler nodded.

"Is there a way across?" Anderson asked.

"There's a small boat tied to the bank, just barely big enough for the three of you. And one hundred paces down the canal there is the remains of a bridge that might be crossed."

At that moment a faint glow came through the windows of the mess as the *Enterprise* dropped out of warp. Mayweather, Anderson, and Cutler scrambled to their feet and went to the windows. Entering a new system was always exciting. Even, Cutler had to admit, better than making up an adventure in their heads.

She glanced over her shoulder. Hoshi clung to the edge of the table, her expression neutral, but her body rigid. She hated any unusual movement of the ship—and she seemed terrified of the changes in speed.

Cutler turned away. The crew had tacitly agreed to ignore Hoshi's reactions, hoping, perhaps, that they would go away.

The yellow sun of the system seemed warm against Cutler's face, even though it wasn't possible to feel heat through the port. A reddish-tinted planet was spinning into view. Greens and blues and reds swam by below them as they dropped into a high orbit.

"Wow, that could be a terraformed Mars," Anderson said.

"Too much water," Mayweather said, pointing at the oceans that covered about a third of the planet.

At that moment Captain Archer's voice came over the communications speakers. "Ensign Hoshi, Ensign Mayweather, report to the bridge."

"We'll start this game later," Anderson said as the two headed for the mess hall door.

"You can count on it," Mayweather said. "After this much setup, I've got to see if we at least can get across the canal."

"Piece of cake," Anderson said, laughing.

Cutler said nothing as she picked up the painted bolts and cup. She knew what she had planned for the three of them crossing the canal. And there wasn't going to be anything easy about it.

TWO

CAPTAIN JONATHAN ARCHER WAS STANDING BESIDE HIS captain's chair, his arm resting on its back, when the sound of the lift caught his attention. It always caught his attention. He was still as excited as a boy about commanding his own starship. Even the word "starship" gave him a slight thrill.

Ensigns Travis Mayweather and Hoshi Sato stepped off the lift. Hoshi's cheeks were dusted a faint pink and she looked down as she moved toward her station. Mayweather had a telltale twinkle in his eye. He'd been teasing her about something, and Hoshi, still uncertain about many things on the ship, provided an easy target.

Archer suppressed a smile as he turned back toward the screen. In experience, in attitude, they were the most different members of his crew. Yet they shared something the rest of the crew did: they were the absolute best at what they did.

The image on the screen caught him and made

him forget his two ensigns. The image of the red and blue and green planet floating there was a beautiful sight. Sometimes he found himself staring at all the new planets, the new space anomalies, with his mouth half open in wonder.

Then he'd catch T'Pol staring at him, and realize he looked like the biggest rube. No wonder she had trouble taking him seriously. The thrill he enjoyed every time he stumbled on a new sight probably seemed like incompetence to her.

He forced himself to take a deep breath and contain the excitement he was feeling. He glanced at the readings in the arm. Everything looked good. They had taken a high orbit over this planet and from what he could tell, there was a decently advanced civilization here.

"I have confirmed a recent warp trail signature," T'Pol said, glancing up at him from her science station. Her dark Vulcan eyes were as intense as always, her expression blank.

A warp trail signature? Really? Finding other aliens was as thrilling to Archer as orbiting a new planet. Maybe more.

"Can you track it?" Archer struggled to sound as dispassionate as T'Pol did. He'd never achieve that, but at least he'd keep the puppylike enthusiasm out of his voice.

"I can," T'Pol said. "It originated from high orbit near the second planet, moved a short distance away, and then terminated."

"A test flight," Archer said, more to himself than anyone.

"That would be a logical deduction," T'Pol said.

"There are a number of satellites and what you might call 'space junk' in low orbit," Lieutenant Malcolm Reed said. "I see nothing threatening."

Archer turned and leaned on the railing separating him from Hoshi. The metal was cold. "Is anyone hailing us?"

"No, sir. There are different radio bands, maybe civilian, maybe not." She raised her head. Her gaze met his. As always, Archer was struck by the brilliance that radiated out of her dark eyes. "Their language is going to be a problem."

"Why's that?" Archer asked.

T'Pol also looked up, from her science station, to wait for Hoshi's answer. The Vulcan's movements were always compact, efficient, in a way that the rest of the crew's weren't. The fact that she raised her head indicated interest.

Archer couldn't imagine Earth's best linguist thinking any language was going to be a problem. Hoshi could almost instantly get a grip on the basics of any tongue. It was the main reason he had desperately wanted her on board for this first trip.

"Structure," Hoshi said. Her head was tilted slightly. She was clearly listening to the aliens' broadcasts as she talked. "I've never heard anything like it. In fact, I've never *imagined* anything like it. The structure of a sentence seems to mean more than the words. At least from what I can gather so far."

Her fingers flew over her board, keying in the computer diagnostic.

"Keep working on it," Archer said. He turned to T'Pol and then Reed. "Well?"

"It appears we've run into a humanoid culture," Reed said, examining the computer screen in front of his station. His fingers pressed buttons as he spoke. "From what I can gather, they're about one hundred years or so behind us technologically."

"Because of a war?" Archer asked, remembering that when the Vulcans discovered Earth a hundred years before, humans were recovering from a very nasty war.

"No," Reed said.

On the main screen the planet below them was in darkness, lights of the cities clear even from this height. Archer couldn't believe their luck. Their mission was to go out and meet new races, and here, almost on their back porch, was a planet just making its first steps into space.

"There is another race on this planet as well," T'Pol said. "They inhabit the southern continent completely."

"What?" Archer said, keying in the scans of the southern continent for the main screen.

It took only a moment before he realized T'Pol was right. Unlike the roads and cities that covered the rest of the planet, this continent seemed almost untouched. Very alien-looking villages dotted the edge of the shoreline all the way around the continent. Thousands and thousands of them, their village structures very different from anything on the rest of the planet. And nowhere near as advanced.

"Are you sure these aren't members of the same race who are just less advanced?" Archer asked. For a long time, humans developed at different rates because of their different cultures. Only recently, historically speaking, had human culture united technologically.

"Yes, I am certain," T'Pol said. Archer thought he caught a bit of a chill in her voice. He'd offended her by questioning her skill. He hadn't been doing that, exactly. He'd just wanted clarification. But he wasn't going to tell her that.

"Captain," Hoshi said, "I'm still not getting all of this language. But I'm pretty certain about a few things."

"Go ahead," Archer said.

"The race that inhabits most of this planet call themselves Fazi." Hoshi paused for a moment, listened, and then shook her head. "They have an extremely structured and rigid society, from what I can tell, and are led by a council of sorts."

"It would be that council we would contact?" Archer asked.

"I think so," Hoshi said.

It was clear to Archer she wasn't one hundred percent sure yet.

"I would recommend patience and study," T'Pol said. "There is much to learn here."

"For the moment I agree," Archer said, dropping into his captain's chair. The leather sank comfortably beneath him, almost as if the chair had been designed to his own physical specs. He leaned forward and studied the planet below as the ship's orbit brought them over the area of sunrise. As he watched, the lights of the alien city below were slowly overwhelmed by the daylight.

Down there people were just waking up and starting their day. Maybe for them it would be a day that would be remembered for a very long time. The day when the Fazi learned there was a much bigger and vaster universe out beyond their solar system. And that they were not alone, just as humanity had learned when the Vulcans landed.

When he took this mission, Archer had promised himself that if—and when—they made first contact, he would do it better than the Vulcans had done.

He intended to keep that promise now.

THREE

ELIZABETH CUTLER WIPED OFF HER TABLE IN THE MESS. She was pleasantly full—having opted for the first night of the homemade stew instead of the Vulcan broth she'd been experimenting with. Everyone said the stew was better the second night, but she still hadn't recovered from her microbiology classes as an undergraduate. Any food that was more than a few hours old had a way of turning her stomach.

She credited that to her imagination. It always forced her to see the microbes forming their little colonies inside what was going to be her meal. The imagined problems got worse when she thought about meat.

Her bolts were resting beside the table, along with a thick towel. She was getting ready to start the game again, although part of her wished she wasn't.

The reddish blue planet floated outside the windows, filling the mess hall with slowly changing colors. Every time the *Enterprise* orbited over different sections of the planet, the colors changed. They had been in high orbit now for over twelve hours.

She'd asked when she had started her duty shift earlier that day if she could start investigating the aliens' biology. But the information they were getting from the planet was too sketchy. Besides, her work was extremely detailed and usually she had to have a sample before she could begin.

She wanted to get down there now and get a sample, but she would have to wait, just like everyone else. Over dinner, Mayweather had confessed that he had the urge to steal a shuttle and head through the planet's atmosphere. He wouldn't do it, of course. None of them would. But she had had the same urge.

So close and yet so far.

Anderson hadn't said much. He'd been spending the day studying the planet's geography and cataloguing the differences between the new planet and Earth. But he was running into the same problems Cutler was. At some point, he'd need to go to the surface to get samples so that he could start a proper geological survey.

But that point wasn't even close yet.

Anderson stood in front of the windows now, his hands clasped behind his back. The air in the mess was close and warm. The environmental systems sometimes couldn't cope with the cooking steam and the increased number of bodies at mealtime. Fortunately, most everyone had finished and left.

Cutler spread her towel over the table and contemplated the game. She'd have to work to make it as interesting as that planet teasing them out there.

She knew there was little chance that Ensign Hoshi would be returning to the role-playing game while they were anywhere near the Fazi planet. From what Cutler had heard, the language of the Fazi had Hoshi pulling out her hair. Cutler couldn't imagine the brilliant woman being upset about anything, but from all reports, Hoshi was getting more and more that way as this language frustrated her at every turn.

Cutler could wait until this real-life drama was over, she supposed, but she didn't want to. She needed to be distracted from her fantasies about the life on the planet below. So she had asked Crewman Alex Novakovich if he'd like to join their first adventure to Mars.

She should have asked him in the first place, but she hadn't thought of it. She avoided thinking about the away mission she had taken with Novakovich. The mission had shaken her to her core, sometimes making her doubt her own mind. If she closed her eyes, she could still see the hallucinations that had so angered her. They had seemed real, even if they were a pollen-induced vision.

Fortunately, Captain Archer was forgiving, and T'Pol, who'd taken the brunt of Cutler's paranoid ravings, said simply that encounters on strange new worlds took tacks that no one expected. *That is why,* she had said, looking at Archer, *Vulcans always proceed with caution.*

Caution was not one of Captain Archer's favorite words—and that was one reason Cutler liked serving under his command.

But as bad as the mission had gone for Cutler, it

had gone even worse for Novakovich. He was still recovering physically from his emergency beam-out in the middle of a sandstorm.

Novakovich had materialized with plants and sticks and sand phased into his skin. The very thought of that experience made Cutler shudder. She'd been giving the transporter a wide berth from the beginning, but that berth was even wider now.

Dr. Phlox had removed all of the larger items, and from what Cutler could tell, the sores were healing well, almost without scars. But, as Novakovich had told her, the sand was causing him the most problems. It had been phased into most of his exposed skin by the transporter, and the only thing Dr. Phlox had been able to do was say that the sand would take care of itself.

"Skin has a way of healing itself," Novakovich had told Culter when she'd expressed surprise at his appearance.

The problem with the sand was that the skin was healing itself by forming pimples around the sand particles and expelling them as whiteheads. (Sand heads? She didn't dare ask, even as a joke.) In all her years, Cutler had never seen such a bad case of acne as Novakovich had. She figured he could use an escape. And he had happily agreed to join the game.

Mayweather came back from dumping his dinner dishes and sat down. "So when do we get this adventure under way?"

For a moment, Cutler thought he was referring to the real planet and the adventure that awaited them.

Then he grabbed his padd and sat in his spot at the table. He meant the Martian adventure, of course.

Anderson left the window and walked back to the table. Novakovich was already seated, studying the weapons information that Anderson had given him during dinner.

"We've got to get Novakovich here a character, first," Cutler said.

Anderson sat down. "I hope yours is less mediocre than mine," he said to Novakovich.

"How come Alex can't use Hoshi's character?" Mayweather asked.

"She might want to rejoin the game at some point," Cutler said. "Besides, it's RPG protocol to roll your own characters."

Mayweather sighed. He clearly wanted to start doing something—inside the adventure game or outside on the planet.

"So," Cutler said to Novakovich, "what's your character's name?"

"Rust," Novakovich said.

"Short for Rusty?" Anderson asked.

"Nope," Novakovich said. "Just Rust. Used to have a dog by that name."

"You might not want an emotional attachment to your character," Cutler said as she handed him the bolts.

"Why not?" Novakovich asked.

"Sometimes characters don't survive adventures."

"I was wondering why we didn't roll a resurrection number," Mayweather said. He was clearly joking.

"In some games you do roll for a number of lives

or resurrections," Cutler said. "But those are *fantasy* role-playing games."

"Yeah," Anderson said, grinning, "and our game is so clearly based in reality."

Cutler smiled. "Let's see who Rust is."

Novakovich dumped the bolts on the table. This time the clatter was muffled by the towel. Cutler was pleased. She wasn't sure she'd be able to handle the sound of metal bolts rolling on a hard tabletop, roll after roll.

Novakovich rolled six red bolts for strength, and nine for intelligence. His charisma came out a dismal three, his dexterity a nine, and his luck a whopping two.

"I don't know who has the worse character, me or you," Anderson said. "Mine is stunningly mediocre, but yours is either bad or good at what he has."

"I think he's typical," Mayweather said. "A smart guy who can't get a girl to save his life."

"Some women like smart men," Cutler said, glancing at Anderson, then looking away. But not before Mayweather caught the look.

"I'm crushed," he said softly, so that only she could hear.

"You're a smart guy," Novakovich said, oblivious of the undertones.

"Oh?" Mayweather said, turning his teasing tone on Novakovich. "Are you saying I can't get a girl either?"

Novakovich shook his head. "Are we ready to play yet or not?"

"Ready," Cutler said. She decided to refresh them

all, since she couldn't remember what she'd told Novakovich. "Here's what you are facing. You have to get a Universal Translator part from a building in the center of the old ruined city. You have landed on the edge of a Martian canal. There are dangerous creatures in the canal, a small boat tied to the shore, or an old bridge."

"Are we working together on this mission?" Novakovich asked.

Cutler shrugged. "Your choice."

She had figured they would, but it wouldn't matter. They could split up if they wanted to. She had asked them to bring padds so they could keep track of where they'd been. If they decided to split up, she wouldn't let them look at each other's padds even though they'd heard the adventure. She would have to modify things slightly if they took a path someone else had walked first.

"I'd like a companion or two," Mayweather said.

"Me, too," Anderson said.

"Who am I to argue?" Novakovich said.

Since they reacted the way the game required, Cutler said nothing. If the other two had disagreed with Mayweather, though, she would have pointed out that he had the highest charisma score now that Hoshi was gone and he would be their leader.

"I vote for the bridge," Anderson said.

"I think I'm with him," Novakovich said.

Mayweather just shrugged, sitting back and smiling. "Why not? I'll go along for the meantime."

"So now we're trudging to the bridge over the sand," Mayweather said. "Right?"

"You've already reached the bridge," Cutler said. She hadn't thought of putting any problems right outside the landing area of the ship. She should have, though. She remembered playing on computer. The best games started with a crisis right up front.

"So what's this bridge like?" Anderson asked.

Cutler glanced at her notes to make sure she was remembering all the details she had worked up right. "The first part of the bridge looks sturdy. But once you get a third of the way across you see a large hole. The hole is too big to jump and the bridge is crumbling away under you."

"So," Anderson said, "let's get a plank long enough to span the hole to make a way across."

"Okay," Cutler said. She glanced at her notes again. She had prepared for this idea. "Where does the plank come from?"

"How should I know?" Anderson said.

"The crumbling part of the bridge," Novakovich said.

"That makes the hole bigger," Cutler said.

"Well, we can't very well take it from the other end," Mayweather said.

She rolled bolts to see if they could dislodge the plank without hurting themselves. They did. She had made this part purposefully easy. Once they set the plank down, she said, "You have a seventy percent chance of making it across."

"I'll go across first," Anderson said.

Cutler handed him the cup of bolts. "Anything more than two red bolts and Mr. Doom makes it."

Anderson nodded and shook the cup, causing a

few nearby diners to glance their way. Then he tipped the cup upside down on the towel.

One red bolt.

Mayweather and Novakovich both burst into laughter.

"Mr. Doom has fallen off the plank and into the water below," Cutler said, also laughing. She glanced at her notes. "Since he has a strength quotient of five, he survived the fall. Now what are you going to do?"

"Swim for shore," Anderson said, not happy with the situation. "And fast."

"Roll the bolts to see if Mr. Doom made it," Cutler said, gathering them up and putting them in the cup. "With a strength quotient of five, Mr. Doom needs a seven or more to make it."

Anderson again shook the cup of bolts and tipped it over the towel.

Three red bolts.

"A mutated Martian canal trout over fifty feet long has seen Mr. Doom swimming, came up and bit him in half," Cutler said. "Mr. Doom is dead."

"Dead?" Anderson asked. He sounded shocked.

"Dead," Cutler said.

Mayweather and Novakovich almost fell off their chairs with laughter.

Anderson kept staring at the three red bolts. "That's not fair. You just wanted Doom out of the game."

"No," Cutler said. "I gave you the odds before you rolled."

"But my character can't *die*."

"She said he could," Mayweather said, his laughter

gone except for that twinkle in his eye. "She said we all could just a few minutes ago."

"I thought she was kidding."

"I don't kid about the rules," Cutler said. "I warned you this was a dangerous mission."

"Just like in real life," Novakovich said. "And I got the pimpled face and sand under my skin to prove it."

That sobered them all, and as a group, they looked at the reddish blue planet taunting them outside the windows.

"Sometimes," Mayweather said, "the risk is worth it."

"Well, the risk isn't worth it to cross a dang bridge on a planet that's wrong for a device that's impossible," Anderson said.

"Your character is just as imaginary as the planet and the bridge," Novakovich said, turning back to the game.

"Yeah," Mayweather said. "Unlike life, you can just roll another one. Right, Elizabeth?"

"Right," she said. "As long as Mayweather and Novakovich don't mind."

"Do it," Mayweather said, waving his hand. "But just don't name him Doom again."

"Fine by me as well," Novakovich said.

Anderson smiled. "All right, how about Dr. Mean?"

As all of them laughed as Cutler rounded up the bolts, put them in the cup, and handed it to Anderson. This was working out better than she had hoped.

"Strength role first," she said.

Anderson's second character, Dr. Mean, had a

strength of six, a dexterity of six, a luck of four, a charisma of five, and an intelligence level of four.

"Dumber than the last one," Mayweather said.

"Yeah," Anderson said, "but I can swim faster."

With that laughter, the game returned to the bridge over the Martian canal, and this time, all three of the adventurers made it across just fine.

FOUR

Captain's log.

For the past half day we have held our position orbiting the planet we are now calling Fazi, for the name of the race of humanoids that inhabits it. To be honest, this waiting is driving me crazy. But at the moment I see no other option. Ensign Hoshi is still not convinced she had a handle on the Fazi language. She's tried to explain it to me twice, but for the moment I'll just let the records of her research speak for themselves. But there's clearly something different about the language.

The Fazi are at an almost identical point in their development as humanity was when the Vulcans stopped by. The only difference that I can see on the surface is that the Fazi did not have to survive any war. That's a good thing, although there seems to be no logical reason for the uneven technological development.

We've also done a number of scans of the other civilization inhabiting the small southern continent of the planet. There is clearly some sort of mutual respect, or treaty, between the two races, since there are no Fazi roads or structures at all on the entire continent.

This other race, which has no sign of any advanced technology beyond basic building of structures, seems to live both on the shore and in the water. We're going to have to get closer before we get clear pictures of them. T'Pol is warning us away from doing just that with either race. So far I have agreed with her, mostly because of Hoshi's problems with the language of the Fazi. But I have to be honest, I'm excited about making this first contact. More excited than I have been in some time.

THE BRIDGE SMELLED OF BEEF STEW AND ARCHER didn't much care. He'd decided that he wanted to eat lunch right in his chair while studying readouts coming in from the planet scans, so he did just that. Captain's prerogative. Besides, when things got interesting, he hated taking the time for a meal and he had learned years ago that if he ate and worked, he would at least stay nourished.

On the big screen in front of him, the Fazi major continent was passing, its greens and reds stark contrasts to the deep blues and white clouds.

Porthos lay on the floor beside the captain's chair,

sleeping, his leg twitching as he chased something in a dream. Archer wished that he could sleep as soundly as his dog sometimes. But that wasn't going to happen any time soon, not as long as they held off first contact with this planet.

Around the bridge everyone worked pretty much in silence. Chief Engineer Charles "Trip" Tucker even had his head stuck under a panel near Hoshi's station, doing adjustments.

"I must say, Captain, I am quite surprised that they haven't seen us up here yet," Lieutenant Reed said, also staring at the screen.

He seemed as fascinated by the planet as Archer was, although his fascination was couched in statements like that one instead of overt enthusiasm. T'Pol seemed to handle Reed's restraint a lot better than Archer's clear excitement.

"However," Reed said, "every bandwidth I check I find nothing mentioning any ship in orbit or referring to a threat from above."

"Societies of this level often do not look to their sky for visitors," T'Pol said. "It is not logical to look when you have no expectation of finding anything."

"Doesn't that assume that they think they're the center of the universe?" Trip asked from underneath the console. "I mean that's not a universal constant, is it? I remember reading about some Earth tribe from a couple hundred years ago that had no word for 'I.' "

"That's right," Hoshi said. "Their language was one of the most fascinating discoveries of its day."

"How can you have conversation if you have no word for 'I'?" Reed asked.

"It's unbelievably difficult," Hoshi said. "Even trying to converse about where you're standing becomes next to impossible. The anthropologists who studied these guys—"

"I'm sure that's fascinating and may even be relevant," Archer said, "but don't you have enough of a linguistic puzzle without explaining an ancient Earth one?"

Hoshi grinned at him from her console. "That's no longer a puzzle, Captain. It's easier to explain something I understand than something I haven't yet figured out."

"That's all right," Archer said, finishing his stew and setting the plate beside the chair. Porthos didn't even wake up. "I don't buy T'Pol's argument anyway. Humans spent a lot of time searching the skies back before the Vulcans arrived."

"You searched for bombs from your enemies," T'Pol said. "And only in low orbits. We are above even that level at the moment. The Fazi would have no reason to see us, other than by chance."

"That doesn't seem quite right to me," Reed said. "After all, they have the ability to go into space. Why would they assume that no one else does?"

"Well, no one else on their planet does," Trip said, taking a different side in the argument.

Archer smiled. Predictably, Trip's vacillation distracted T'Pol.

"I thought you believed that my argument was incorrect," she said.

"Never said that." Trip's hand appeared in the aisle

and groped for another tool, not finding it. "The captain said that."

"I didn't say it was incorrect," Archer said, suppressing a grin. "I said I didn't buy it."

"Well, I'm beginning to buy it," Hoshi said. "This society is more structured than anything I could have ever imagined developing. In fact I have no idea why it did, but that's for later research."

"Okay, I missed the connection," Archer said. "What does being structured have to do with not seeing us?"

Beside him, Porthos grunted and rolled over. He licked his chops, but his eyes were still closed.

"Because," Hoshi said, bending down to hand Trip the tool he'd been groping for, "for them to look for us, it would have to have been planned, carefully, and in great detail."

"Now you lost me," Archer said.

"Yeah, me too," Trip said, coming out from under the board and closing up the panel. "How can you plan to look for something you don't know exists?"

"Exactly," Hoshi said as she turned from her panel to face Archer and the rest of the bridge crew. "Every sentence of their language has an exact structure. And the structure dictates meaning of the sentence, sometimes even more than the words. Two words simply inverted can change the entire meaning of a phrase."

"Got that much," Archer said, "but I'm not following why that would mean they wouldn't see us up here."

"There is only one word for anything they do," Hoshi said, "unlike most Earth languages, which often have two or three or more words for any given act."

Archer motioned for her to get on with her idea.

"Every word the Fazi use has an exact meaning. It seems to me that every single thought of these people is controlled by the structure of their language."

"I thought that's how all languages worked," Trip said. "We're always trying to overcome our preconceived notions as expressed in our language."

Archer raised an eyebrow. Occasionally Trip dropped his rough-edged Southerner exterior and showed the intelligence that lurked beneath. He usually didn't realize when he'd done it.

"Yes and no," Hoshi said. "Most languages adapt to change quickly—inventing new terms or adopting them from other languages. I'm not even sure this one can do that. The Fazi language structure, from what T'Pol and Reed have discovered, also carries through to every detail in the Fazi world. Right?"

"It does seem that way," Reed said. "The roads are uniform. The cities are perfectly laid out, and the patterns of repetition of services are everywhere. Even their broadcasts are exact and very structured."

"And in all the broadcasts we've listened to, and that we have scanned," Hoshi said, "we haven't found one word about art, or one note of music, or one mention of a sport."

"How dull," Reed said.

"No kidding," Trip said.

"You'd think they'd play games," Archer said. "Games are structured."

"But the outcomes are not," T'Pol said. "My research shows that this culture believes in control and precision. An unexpected outcome violates their sense of structure."

"So unless it was planned to look at this exact location in the sky, no one would do so?" Archer asked.

"That would be my guess," Hoshi said.

"Makes Vulcan society look downright free-form," Trip said, then laughed at the blank stare from T'Pol.

Archer sat back and stared at the images of the planet rotating past on the screen. "Seems we're about ready for a first contact."

"I would strongly advise against it," T'Pol said.

"Why?" Archer asked, glancing back at the Vulcan subcommander.

"For precisely the reasons we discussed," T'Pol said. "A first contact might violate their sense of structure."

"They've got to be able to deal with surprises," Archer said. "No one's life can be planned to the nanosecond."

"You are making an assumption," T'Pol said. "We do not have enough information to make such a contact successful."

"What more do we need?" Archer asked. "We know they are not threatening or dangerous in any fashion. They are starting to work toward real space-flight by testing warp engines. And we know they love set structure in their world. It would seem to me that your people didn't know much more about us."

"I'm afraid, Captain," Hoshi said, "I have to agree with T'Pol. I'm just not secure enough on all the details of the Fazi language to guarantee success."

Archer stared at Hoshi, then back at T'Pol.

"All right," Archer said, sighing and turning back

to sit facing the big screen. "You've all got another twenty-four hours and I'll decide then, if they haven't already spotted us before then."

"Perfect," Trip said. "I got three different tests I can run."

"Just make sure to keep us ready to move if we have to," Archer said.

"Oh, trust me," Trip said as he headed for the lift, "we're more than ready to move."

The sound of licking came from the floor below. Porthos was no longer asleep. He was finishing the stew in Archer's bowl.

"Porth—oh, never mind," Archer said. After all, he'd set the bowl there. As far as Porthos was concerned, anything on the floor with food in it belonged to him. Archer had never disabused him of that notion.

Archer looked back up at the planet. He wanted to go down there so badly he vibrated with it. However, for the moment, it made more sense to trust his officers and their judgment. But controlling his own excitement about making a first contact with the Fazi was becoming harder and harder.

He picked up his bowl. Porthos looked at him expectantly. "Come on, boy," Archer said. "Let's go for a walk. I think we both need it."

As he left the bridge, he glanced at the other officers. All three hovered over their scanning equipment, lost in the search for information.

FIVE

THE LAUGHING AND THE BOLTS BANGING ON THE TABLE had either driven the remaining crew members from the mess area or brought them over to watch. Those who did watch wanted to give advice, and Cutler wouldn't allow it. She did offer them a chance to roll up and sit down, but she insisted that they'd have to start where the ship touched down instead of joining the adventure in progress.

Everyone declined, and one by one the kibitzers left.

The planet slowly displayed its colors outside the windows, intriguing in its strangeness. Cutler was used to seeing Earth—the big blue and white mass against the blackness of space—but she wasn't used to the hints of red, the shape of the continents, the way the clouds formed over this distinct ball.

She caught herself looking at it from time to time, remembering that there were other adventures in her life—real adventures, just waiting to be had.

"Waiting" was the key word. No one had told her that patience would be a virtue in space.

But the game was helping her, Mayweather, Anderson, and Novakovich kill time. Except for the loss of Anderson's first character, Mr. Doom, things had gone along smoothly. The players had managed to make it across the bridge and through a crossing in a road that had traps. Novakovich's player, Rust, had used one hand-grenade-like bomb to clear out a roadblock, and it had worked. Otherwise, all three players still had their full ammunition and weapons.

"Now you're approaching the outskirts of the ruined Martian city," Cutler said, describing the scene that faced them. "The main road in front of you goes between tall buildings, with lots of debris in the street. There is a staircase entrance on the right side of the street that goes down into a subway system."

"What about going up?" Anderson asked. He was proving her most inquisitive and competitive player. "Are the buildings connected?"

Cutler tried not to show her surprise. She had designed the path into the city to have three main routes, underground, surface, and through the connecting bridges between the buildings. But she hadn't planned on telling the players about the connecting bridges unless they asked. And she hadn't expected anyone to ask so soon.

"The buildings are connected by sky bridges in most cases," Cutler said, "Some of the sky bridges are in need of repair, just as the rest of the buildings in this ruined old city are."

The players sat in silence for a moment, all clearly

thinking. Novakovich checked his padd as if it gave him answers about where he was going. All it did, of course, was tell him where he'd been. He was the only one who assiduously followed her advice to map their progression. The others had dropped that suggestion in the game's first real hour.

Finally Mayweather said, "I vote we stay together and stay on the ground."

"Why?" Anderson asked. "Seems to me going up would be the safest way."

"We can always go inside and up," Mayweather said. "I think we should make as much ground out in the open, where we can see what's coming at us."

"Yeah," Novakovich said. "I like that idea. Rust is sticking with Unk."

"Sounds good to me," Anderson said. "Dr. Mean is with Unk as well. Let's go in on the ground."

Cutler sighed with relief. So far, these guys worked well as a team. She remembered from her childhood days players who squabbled about every fork in the road. In fact, she remembered that better than she remembered the rules.

Maybe these players worked well together in the game because they had to in real life. They knew the value of teamwork, even if no one was directly in charge.

"Ahead of you one block is a large pile of what looks to be wrecked transportation vehicles," Cutler said, looking at her notes. "These vehicles are long and narrow, and were designed to carry a lot of passengers. The pileup fills most of the street."

"Lots of options now," Anderson said, rubbing his

hands together. "We can try to go over, we can go down a side street, in either direction, or into a building."

"How about through the pile?" Mayweather asked.

"Through?" Novakovich asked.

"Sure," Mayweather said, smiling at Cutler. "You said these were long and narrow. Can we go through the pile?"

"You can try," Cutler said. She was trying to be mysterious. She noted that, earlier in the game, she had given away the best route just through her tone of voice.

"Unk's going through," Mayweather said.

"Lead the way," Anderson said.

"Rust is right behind you."

Cutler checked her notes again. These three were getting off to a pretty good start, at least so far. She had planned that if they did try to go through, they would meet one blocked door. She told them about the transport door that was stuck closed.

"Rust is the strongest," Novakovich said. "Any harm in trying to just pull it open?"

"None," Cutler said, "but it won't open. You would have to have someone with a strength of at least eight to budge it."

"Where's Hoshi's character when you need her?" Anderson asked.

"Waiting, just like we are, while she's having a real adventure," Mayweather said.

The players glanced at the planet again. It dominated the mess hall, which had grown colder as people left. The smell of dinner was finally receding as well, although the acrid scent of the soap used on the dishes still remained.

"I'm not real sure Hoshi's considering her difficulties an adventure," Anderson said.

"Yeah," Novakovich said. "I hear she's been having some real troubles with this one."

"I thought she was some kind of genius when it came to language," Anderson said. "How come she can't get this one?"

"Maybe for the same reason she said there couldn't be a Universal Translator. Maybe the languages she knows and the language these Fazi speak don't have enough commonalities," Cutler said, feeling the need to defend Hoshi.

"You'd think they would," Mayweather said. "I mean, she knows more languages than anyone I've ever heard of."

Cutler nodded as Novakovich rubbed at his face with the heel of his hand. Clearly Dr. Phlox had told him not to scratch, and just as clearly Novakovich's sand pimples itched.

"Well, you guys don't have Hoshi anymore," Novakovich said, "and Rust only has a strength of six. So we have to figure out how to open this door."

Cutler gave him a grateful smile. She was glad to return to the game, even though she shot one last look at the planet.

"How about blowing the door open?" Anderson asked.

"Possible," Cutler said, still using her mysterious voice.

"And the chance of bringing the entire wreckage down on top of us?" Mayweather asked.

"Also possible." She smiled at Mayweather and didn't tell him just how likely that was, since characters in this situation wouldn't know.

"I think we should just turn back and go around," Novakovich said. "Try a side street."

Mayweather nodded, but Anderson wasn't so sure. "You two go back outside the wreckage and wait. I'll set the grenade and run. I have four seconds, don't I?"

Cutler nodded. The grenades they were carrying in this game did have that kind of delay.

"Good, I should be mostly out of the wreckage by the time it blows."

"You going to try that?" Cutler asked, sounding more anxious than she planned. She tried not to look alarmed that she had once again indicated their course.

Mayweather glanced at her, his brown eyes missing nothing. She made sure she didn't meet his gaze. Instead, she looked at her notes. She would have to adjust slightly for Anderson running to escape the blast, but not much else from what she had worked out.

"Sure," Anderson said.

"Your luck score isn't very high," Mayweather said to Anderson.

Cutler waited. If Mayweather, as Unk, asked Anderson, as Dr. Mean, to abandon this idea, she'd have to roll to see if Anderson could follow that advice. Chances were that Dr. Mean couldn't stand up to Unk's charisma.

Anderson shrugged. "It's higher than Novakovich's."

"And look at me," Novakovich said with a grin. He rubbed his cheek with the inside of his wrist.

"I don't think anyone rolled a luck score for the transporter device," Cutler said.

"Oh, I think they did," Novakovich said. "And I think I was real lucky. What if the thing had stuck my arm where my nose should be?"

"You'd have a heck of a time seeing the table," Anderson said.

"Nothing fazes you, does it?" Novakovich said.

"Oh, yeah," Mayweather said. "He gets fazed fairly often. He likes to pretend he's cooler than he is."

Anderson gave him a pretend-mean glare. Mayweather grinned.

"What are you guys doing about that door?" Cutler asked, ready to get back to the game.

"Unk will be waiting outside," Mayweather said, "against a building under cover, just to be safe."

Novakovich nodded. "Rust is with Unk."

"Dr. Mean is blowing and running," Anderson said.

Cutler picked up the cup of bolts and tipped them out. "There's a fifty percent chance the explosion will collapse the wreckage."

Three red bolts.

"The wreckage collapsed," Cutler said.

She gathered up the bolts and handed them to Anderson. "Dr. Mean has a strength of six, and adding in two points for the running, anything eight or under will mean he got out safely."

"Come on, Dr. Mean, run your butt off," Anderson said as he dumped the bolts out on the towel.

Four red bolts.

"Yes, safe with plenty of room to spare," Anderson said.

Mayweather let out a large breath, obviously relieved. His gaze met Cutler's again, and she could tell what he was thinking. He didn't really want Anderson to lose a second character in the same night.

Cutler smiled at her players. "However, the explosion has drawn the attention of the Martians. Ten of them are coming down the street at your position now."

"Oh, just great," Mayweather said, shaking his head at Anderson. "Now you've done it. Remind me to never go on a real away mission with you."

"I'm a lot more circumspect in real life," Anderson said.

"Somehow," Novakovich said so softly only Cutler could hear, "I doubt that."

SIX

Captain's log.

Under recommendation from both T'Pol and Hoshi, I've agreed to wait another twenty-four hours before deciding to make the first contact with the Fazi. Can't say as I like the waiting, but I suppose this time it is the best course. Hoshi believes that if the Fazi language is any indication of their culture, they will be more structured than any organization ever put together on Earth. She thinks they might even be more controlled than the Vulcans, which I find hard to imagine.

Fortunately, T'Pol has shown some restraint. I think we're both aware that the Enterprise now finds itself in the same position with the Fazi that the Vulcans were in with Earth. She watches me closely, expecting me to ask for her advice. If anything, I'll make new mistakes, but I won't repeat the old.

Twenty-two hours from now, we'll see which method is better. In the meantime, I hope to get a few good meals, a good night's sleep, and do a little studying on what we have learned about the Fazi so that we can put Earth's best foot forward.

"HOSHI, WOULD YOU LIKE TO SEE JUST HOW FAR THE Fazi take structure?" Reed asked, staring at the image he had just come up with.

The bridge was quiet. T'Pol had gone to rest, and Captain Archer had not come back since he had given them twenty-four hours to find more information about the Fazi. That left Reed with the bridge command, Hoshi at communications, and junior staff manning the other stations, all working scanning equipment of some sort trying to gather as much information as possible.

Hoshi moved over to the screen Reed was using. She stepped delicately beside him. He could see the tension in her hands as she braced her fingers on the lip of the control panel. Earlier, the captain had ordered her to take a meal break. Soon, Reed suspected, the captain would have to order her to sleep or she'd collapse from exhaustion and overstimulation.

"What would you like me to see?" she asked.

On the screen he had put a map of the main northern continent where the Fazi capital was. It seemed to have been built in the center of the landmass and other, lesser cities radiated out from it. That pattern was what first caught Reed's eye.

He backed up the image and made a blinking dot appear on the Fazi council chambers. "This," he said, "is the center of their universe."

"Seems that way." Hoshi leaned in and stared at his screen.

"Using the council chambers as the center," Reed said, "I ran radiant lines, like spokes on a wheel, outward every ten degrees. Thirty-six lines. Do you see?"

He tapped on his control board and the blue lines appeared, moving out from the council chamber location.

"I have stopped them at the edge of the continent, but this still works if you take them all the way around."

"Okay." Hoshi glanced at her station. He could feel her impatience to return to the linguistic challenge.

"Next," he said, "I added circles around the center, moving out one degree at a time."

Reed punched another key and red circles appeared on the map, growing larger and larger as they moved outward.

"Now," he said, "let's superimpose a map of the Fazi roads and cities on my wheel diagram."

Leaving the blue and red lines, he placed the Fazi cities and major roads over the lines.

"Oh, my . . ." Hoshi said.

"Startling, isn't it?" Reed said. "All major roads, without exception, are on one of those lines. One would think there would be at least one deviation."

"One would think," Hoshi said, her ear catching

his accent and repeating it slightly. She probably wasn't even aware she had done it.

Reed traced a line with his finger, amazed at the feat of construction and control this meant. "All cities are built at the corners, with the exact centers of the cities being the point of intersection. This is, without a doubt, the most amazing feat of construction I have ever seen, or even imagined."

"If their cities are this regimented," Hoshi said, "imagine their lives."

"Yes, well," Reed said, and didn't continue. He had been imagining it. He liked order in his life—a great deal of it, actually—but not as much as this map indicated. He also liked unpredictability and adventure, or he would never have joined the *Enterprise* crew.

"Why would any civilization develop this kind of phobia about control and order?" Hoshi asked.

"I have no idea," Reed said. "It is clear, however, that this entire civilization was carefully built or, perhaps we should say, rebuilt since we do not know the history of this place."

"It's the same with their language. Why that much structure? What would cause this?"

"I believe we must discover the answer to that question before Captain Archer can go meet them."

Hoshi frowned. "I doubt he's going to wait that long."

"I know he's not," Reed said. He looked back at the lines, and shuddered.

SEVEN

THROUGH THE MESS HALL WINDOWS, THE PLANET STILL loomed, but even when Cutler glanced up, she no longer saw it. The mess itself, with its dark walls and bright lighting, almost seemed invisible.

Instead, in her mind's eye, she saw the ruined Martian city she had invented, the destroyed transport vehicles lining the road, and the buildings crumbling around her. She could almost smell the red dust and feel the blistering heat. Humid heat, she figured, because of the canals.

It seemed like Mayweather, Anderson, and Novakovich could see the landscape as well. They were all leaning forward, calling out their actions as if they were actually taking them. The battle between their three intrepid explorer characters and the evil remnants of the Martian civilization loomed.

"The Martians are coming! The Martians are coming!" Mayweather shouted, managing to keep his expression serious while he leaned back in his chair.

"Pull back to cover," Novakovich said, just as he would have if he were really on the planet. "What kind of cover do we have available?"

"There's a building open on your right," Cutler said, "and piles of rubble along the left side of the street."

"Building!" both Novakovich and Anderson said at the same time.

"The Martians are coming," Mayweather said again. He was almost singing the words. Then he froze as he too got caught in the game. "What are they armed with?"

"Long knives, sharp claws, sharp teeth," Cutler said.

"Poison in their bites, I bet," Mayweather said.

"I wouldn't give you much chance of survival if you're bit by one," Cutler said, sorry that he was ahead of her again.

"How many are there?" Anderson asked.

"A dozen," Cutler said.

"Hold your fire," Mayweather said, "until you see the green of their eyes."

"They're closing in," Culter said.

"Can we see the green of their eyes?" Mayweather asked.

"I don't know," Cutler said. "We haven't rolled to see how good your vision is."

Anderson gave her a withering look, then said, "Fire now!"

"Firing," Novakovich said.

"Shoot low, Sheriff," Mayweather said, "the Martians are riding ponies."

Cutler looked at the young pilot. "What?"

"Old joke," Mayweather said, waving the explanation away. "My father told it to me."

She shook her head at him. The joke had broken the illusion for her. The mess hall's chill had vanished, though, in all the excitement.

"You know I'm firing too, don't you?" Mayweather asked.

"Now I do," Cutler said as she rolled the bolts.

"Did we stop them?" Anderson asked.

Cutler stared at the bolts. Eight red. Eight times three meant the dozen Martians were more than stopped. "Mowed them down."

"But I bet all the noise is going to bring more," Anderson said.

"No doubt in my mind," Mayweather said. "I'm sure Cutler still has a few tricks up her sleeve."

Cutler smiled. That was exactly what a game master liked to hear. "You're right," she said to Anderson. "Martian reinforcements are on the way."

"How many?" Novakovich asked.

"You can't tell yet," Cutler said.

"No fair," Anderson said.

"It's a game, James," Cutler said. "No one ever said anything about fair."

"We need some kind of device that lets us read things far away. How come you didn't give us one?" Mayweather said.

"For exactly this reason," Cutler said.

"How far away are they?" Novakovich asked.

Cutler shrugged. "If you can't see them, you have no idea. I just confirmed your guess. Now I'm kind of sorry I did, since there's no way you'd know they were coming."

"We figured it out," Anderson said. "You didn't give anything away."

She did, but she wasn't going to say any more. She should have let them continue with their suppositions, hit them with a few other hidden surprises and made them forget about the Martians, and then had the Martian reinforcements attack. Next time. It would all be easier on the next game.

"How much ammunition do we have left?" Anderson asked.

Good question. She wondered if anyone would get to that.

"You used one-quarter of your rounds," Cutler said.

"I'd say this would be a good time to get my favorite alien Unk into a building," Mayweather said. "You two coming?"

"Right behind you," Anderson said.

"Rust is with you as well," Novakovich said.

"Which building are you going into?" Cutler said. She had a timer going on her padd, but she didn't tell them that. If they continued to play the game in real time, they only had fifteen minutes until the second wave of Martians attacked.

"Which building. She asks us which building." Mayweather rolled his eyes. "The closest one, of course."

"Yeah," Anderson said.

Discipline was breaking down in the ranks. Cutler suppressed a grin. If anyone talked to the captain like that on an away mission, there'd be trouble.

"All right," Cutler said. "You find a big room inside the closest building. The room's mostly dark, but you have enough light to see a wide, open ramp leading up to a second floor."

"Let's go up," Anderson said.

The other two nodded.

"Second floor looks much like the first. Windows are missing and the holes give you more light, so you can see the garbage and rubble mounding around the floor. A ramp leads up to the third floor."

"For the moment we're safe," Mayweather said.

Cutler laughed.

Mayweather looked alarmed at her laugh. Clearly he was getting the rhythm of the game. "Safe" was a relative—and short—term in this RPG.

"Are we safe enough to take a break until after our shifts?" Mayweather asked. "I got to get some sleep. Fighting these Martians is tiring."

"Good idea." Novakovich glanced at Cutler. "You and I both have duty in seven hours."

"I suppose your characters are safe enough for that," Cutler said, laughing. She put the bolts back in the cup, wrapped the towel around it, and stood as the others did. It was amazing how quickly time went by with this crazy game. Just as it had when she was a kid, playing it on her computer. Only linking minds, as they were doing now, seemed to be a lot more fun than linking computers.

And it was nice to be playing with people who cooperated with each other instead of fighting among themselves.

EIGHT

THE TENSION ON THE BRIDGE WAS THICK, BOTH FROM excitement and worry. Archer strolled around his captain's chair, unable to keep still. He'd left Porthos in his quarters, knowing that the next few hours would be difficult.

The bridge crew watched him pace. Twenty-two hours had passed since Archer had promised them twenty-four more hours. He'd planned to stay off the bridge for the entire twenty-four so that the crew could do their research and studies, but he hadn't been able to. He needed to know what was going on.

The reports had come at him fast, filled with information. He processed it quickly too, hating the discussion that inevitably came when he allowed the crew to interact during this time. He'd vowed not to hold briefings, and so far he'd been able to stick to it, even when he had to use unorthodox methods, like this one.

The staff was used to more organization and a

captain who didn't pace. T'Pol in particular found his methodology difficult. Even though they'd declared a truce of sorts, she still made him nervous. Right now she served as a reminder of all that the Vulcans had withheld from the humans.

He wasn't going to do that to the Fazi.

The only two people with nothing to report were Mayweather, who looked as if he hadn't gotten enough sleep, sitting at the pilot's station, and Trip, leaning on the wall beside the lift door. Trip was the only one who didn't seem on edge. In fact, he was watching Archer with something akin to amusement.

Apparently the Fazi were more structured than anyone could have imagined. Their civilization, built on a perfect grid pattern, amazed Archer even more than the structure to their language Hoshi had tried to explain to him.

When the reports were finished, Archer stopped pacing and looked at T'Pol. "Do you think that the Fazi colonized this world at some point in their past? And that the race on the southern continent was here first?"

"It would be a possible answer to the Fazi engineering puzzle," T'Pol said. "Building on such a pattern would be more logical if done from the beginning of a settlement. Also, the Fazi seem quite different from the race on the southern continent—not just in technological advancement, but physically as well."

"Is it unusual for two such different species to develop on the same planet?" Archer asked.

T'Pol opened her mouth to answer him, and then stopped, recognizing his trap. He wanted her to tell him information he wasn't supposed to have.

"Since we have discovered few similarities be-tween these two cultures," T'Pol said, carefully avoid-ing his overall question, "it would be logical to assume that one group originated somewhere else."

"I'm not so sure," Hoshi said.

"About which part?" Archer asked.

"The structure," she said. "I think we're making as-sumptions based on who we are. Sure, we tend to be more structured when we colonize, but some crea-tures are innately structured, like ants."

Archer glanced at T'Pol. She was watching Hoshi, her features impassive. Without meaning to, Hoshi had insulted T'Pol. It wasn't the challenge to her as-sumption that was the insult; rather, it was the impli-cation that T'Pol had extrapolated from a narrow perspective instead of the open one she subscribed to.

"I'll grant you innate structure," Archer said. "But how can we be sure these people have it?"

"Their language," Hoshi said. "It tells me that everything about them is structured. It would then make sense that such structure would carry over into their world building, even if grown into."

"But why have such structure in the first place?" Archer asked.

No one suggested an answer to him, which told him clearly that no one even had the foggiest clue.

"All right," he said, taking a different tack, "is there any obvious reason why the Fazi are not on the southern continent with that other race?"

"The two races are incompatible." T'Pol keyed in something on her board and nodded toward the main screen. It showed a high-level shot of one of the alien villages. "It would seem the residents of this village are able to live both on land and in the water."

"The images that I have studied of the creatures of the southern continent show them to be crab- or spiderlike." Reed seemed to be pausing for effect. "However, they are the size of cows."

In spite of himself, Archer shuddered. "Spiders the size of cows?"

Reed shrugged.

"I'll volunteer to stay behind when you go on that away mission," Trip said.

"I would suggest that no contact with such a primitive race be made at this time," T'Pol said.

"Fine by me." Archer didn't like the idea of having to talk with a spider that big. He paced for a moment behind his chair, then stopped and faced T'Pol. "I assume you have objections to making first contact with the Fazi?"

"I do," she said. "This is a complex culture that needs more study."

"How much more?" Archer asked.

"If we continue working as intensely as we have these past twenty-two hours, nine minutes, and seven seconds," T'Pol said, "it would take at least six days, perhaps longer."

"Perhaps longer," Archer repeated, wondering how she even came to her figures. Maybe she was just using the Vulcan template.

"There are nuances in this language that may take me months to figure out," Hoshi said.

Archer smiled. "You've worried about the nuances

in all the new languages you've been learning. You haven't harmed us yet."

Hoshi did not smile back. "I have not come across a language this detailed before."

"I don't plan on having us sit here in orbit for a week or more." The very idea of it gave Archer the shivers. He turned to Hoshi. "Ensign, can you program the translators with this language well enough to be understood?"

"Well enough to be understood, yes, but—"

"Do you have the translators programmed?"

"As much as I can, sir," Hoshi said.

Archer nodded. His mind had been made up before he came on the bridge and he knew it. Nothing T'Pol or Hoshi or Reed had shown him had convinced him otherwise.

"Okay, Trip, get a shuttlepod prepped and ready to go. Hoshi, I want you and Reed and Trip on this one. Mayweather, you're driving. T'Pol, you have the bridge. We go in two hours."

"Sir," Hoshi said, "I'm going to need a little time to prepare you for this language and the structure involved."

Archer laughed. "You can always bail me out if I stumble or stutter."

"No, sir, I can't," Hoshi said. "Having an inferior speak out of turn at such an event as this would cause serious harm and might be a fatal breach of protocol for the Fazi. There is no telling what might happen."

Archer looked at her. She was clearly serious and worried. "All right, Ensign, you can prepare me, but in the captain's mess. I need something to eat."

"Sir," T'Pol said, "I would suggest one more thing."

Archer stopped and looked at the Vulcan subcommander. "Yes?"

"I would send the Fazi a message, stating your intention of landing at a certain point, at a certain exact time, and then request an audience with their council."

"You want me to call ahead and make an appointment?" Archer asked. "For a first contact?"

"In a matter of speaking," T'Pol said.

"It would be a very good idea, sir," Hoshi said. "Remember how structured they are."

Archer shook his head. He had always figured that first contacts would be different and interesting, but he had never imagined anything like this. "T'Pol, make the call. Unless you believe I should do it."

"No, sir. Given their cultural hierarchy, it would not be advisable for you to do such a task," T'Pol said.

Again Hoshi nodded.

For the first time, he was starting to wonder if this was such a good idea after all. The tension on the bridge grew even thicker than it had been.

Still, a first contact awaited. He grinned. "Come on, people. We're out here to meet new people. I'd say it's about time we met the Fazi, up close and personal. Two hours."

"All right!" Trip said, clapping his hands before turning and heading into the lift. "Road trip."

Archer smiled at his chief engineer. Having him be excited balanced the caution and fear coming from Hoshi and T'Pol.

An hour later, after having Hoshi lecture him over the dos and don'ts of the Fazi language and Fazi customs while he tried to choke down a bowl of chicken soup, Archer had lost almost all his excitement. Now he felt more like an actor climbing on a stage with only half his lines memorized.

He wondered if the Vulcans had felt that way when talking to humans for the first time.

Then he remembered: Vulcans claimed not to feel anything.

For the first time, he thought them lucky.

NINE

ARCHER FORCED HIMSELF TO LOOK THROUGH THE shuttlepod's windows as Mayweather guided it through the atmosphere. Archer longed to take the controls himself, pilot the shuttlepod to its landing, and then step out, being the first to touch Fazi soil.

He wouldn't, though. As much as he wanted to do everything himself, he knew better. This first contact would be a joint mission, and it would go as smoothly as possible.

The shuttlepod was suddenly engulfed by blue sky.

"Gotta love that," Trip said, sinking back in his seat.

"It is the differences that intrigue," Reed said, peering through his own window.

Next to Archer, Hoshi shifted slightly in her seat. She had been nervous from the moment the shuttlepod had left the *Enterprise*. At first, Archer had attributed that to her nervousness about anything to do with space travel, but now he was beginning to think he was wrong.

"Sir," she said, "I think we should circle once."

Archer was about to ask why and then he noted the time on the digital display before him. They were early.

He glanced at Hoshi. Her entire body was rigid. If she thought it was that important to land exactly on time, then they would land exactly on time.

"Make a big wide circle on the glide path, Ensign," Archer said to Mayweather.

Mayweather seemed to be enjoying himself. The long fingers of his left hand pushed buttons while the palm of his right rested on the steering lever Mayweather sometimes called a joystick.

"You got it, sir," Mayweather said. "I'll make sure we touch down exactly on the appointed time."

Hoshi still looked worried.

"It's going to work out," Archer said. "You'll see."

She nodded, and he could tell she was unconvinced. The shuttlepod circled over the Fazi central city. Archer wondered if the Fazi were looking up and watching them.

Perhaps they needed an appointment for that as well.

"Wow, talk about cookie-cutter construction," Trip said. "Everything is built exactly the same."

"It does save on materials," Reed said. "Not to mention the fact that you must train your labor force only once."

Archer took his attention off his crew and looked out over the impressive expanse of Fazi city. It was so perfectly organized that there were patterns in everything. Even the roofs had all the chimneys in the exact same locations, which meant, more than likely, that every house the same size was designed and laid out inside exactly the same way. For Archer, who had trouble at times keeping things in their right place in his small quarters, this was just about as alien as it came.

Hoshi had prepped the team on how they were to act, right down to what positions they were to stand in and how Archer was to introduce everyone. But she had warned him a few times that there was still a great deal about this language and culture she didn't understand, the largest being why it had developed in this fashion.

He believed the development mattered less than she did. Since she understood the language and had enough understanding of the culture to know the details of protocol, she was prepared enough. The history would come later.

"We'll land in five seconds," Mayweather said as the shuttlepod turned and lowered itself down toward an empty mall area near the capitol building.

This had been the agreed-upon landing site. The mall reminded Archer of the parks he loved in San Francisco. Large expanses of green, planned walkways surrounded by blooming plants. However, here the walkways did not curve, and the plants repeated in a pattern just like everything else.

The actual landing surface was in the exact center of the mall—a wide brick area that had obviously been designed for just such a purpose.

"Good job," Archer said.

Behind him Hoshi let out a deep sigh of relief that echoed in the shuttlepod.

Mayweather laughed. "Thanks for the vote of confidence. I didn't think my flying was that bad."

"It's not," Hoshi said. "It's just—"

"It's okay," Mayweather said. "I know how you feel about flying."

She smiled at him, but the tension hadn't left her. Archer studied her without turning his head. For once, her nervousness over flying had been overshadowed by her nervousness about something else.

The first contact.

Was she this worried because this was her very first mission of this type, or was she that insecure about the language? He had trouble reading her reactions sometimes. Hoshi's general caution was foreign to him, and he couldn't understand it as easily as he liked.

"Trust me," Trip said, laughing, "I sometimes feel the same way."

Archer laughed, then glanced at his watch. "Let's go, folks. Stay in the order and the formation Hoshi laid out for us."

Mayweather moved out of his chair and opened the shuttlepod hatch. The air was warm, slightly humid, and smelled of jasmine. After the last few weeks inside the ship, the fresh air felt wonderful.

"Nothing like the smell of an alien planet's air in the morning," Trip said. "Don't you just love it?"

Everyone sat for a moment, letting the silence and fresh air flow in over them. Much as he loved the ship, Archer liked this feeling as well. If he concentrated, he could sense the differences from Earth.

The air smelled of jasmine, yes, but something else, something unfamiliar, almost spicy. He knew nothing smelled like that on Earth. And the oxygen content of the air was slightly different, which T'Pol had warned them about. Not different enough to make the air unbreathable—just different enough to be alien.

Archer wondered if he could sense that too, or if he was reacting to it because T'Pol had told him about the difference.

He could analyze the details of this place forever, but he didn't have time. He stood. "Okay, let's stay focused here. We have a first contact to make."

Fazi protocol was similar to protocol in old Earth aristocracies. The leader, contrary to his name, never went first. The junior ranking officials led the way, probably in case of danger. Archer smiled. As if danger bothered him.

As the junior member of the team, Mayweather climbed out first and stepped to one side, his heels shushing on the bricks. It was amazingly quiet here. No bird noises or animal sounds. No insect buzzes or traffic noise.

Archer found the silence unnerving.

Hoshi went out next and stepped to the other side. Then Reed, then Trip, and finally Archer.

As Hoshi had instructed them to do, Archer got out and, without a look or a word to the others, started across the courtyard. Finally he got to lead.

The capitol building's shape was similar to all the other buildings they'd seen from the air. Only this building was larger. From the air, the buildings had looked white, but on closer inspection, he realized that they were a reddish white, almost a pale pink.

Two-story square columns held up a balcony that lined the third floor. The columns were made of the same brick as the walkway. The bricks were amazingly uniform. Archer had seen old brick on Earth, and knew that the bricks crumbled or were sometimes molded to slightly different shapes. But not here. Each brick was the same size and there was no sign of crumbling.

There was also no sign of life.

Were all the Fazi in hiding or did they not believe in guards? He felt disconcerted. Somehow he had expected a more formal greeting upon their arrival.

Trip fell in to his right, a step behind, showing his rank of second-in-command.

Reed was next, on Archer's left, a step behind Trip.

Hoshi and Mayweather were another step behind Reed on either side, staying even with each other.

Archer could feel that they were being watched from a thousand different places in the buildings that surrounded the plaza, yet there wasn't a Fazi in sight. It would have been much more natural, in a public plaza of this size, to have crowds around. This way he felt exposed and vulnerable.

Both T'Pol and Hoshi had assured him there was no need to take weapons. They both were convinced there was no chance the Fazi would turn violent. Hoshi had even said that the chaos of war or violence could never be allowed in a culture this structured. Maybe that was why it had developed this way. Personally, he'd take the chance of war in exchange for personal freedom, music, and art.

When he reached the square columns, the wide doors to the council chambers opened. The Fazi had said the doors would open at a specific time. Apparently, the *Enterprise* team was right on schedule. Archer never broke stride, moving inside as if he had been here a dozen times before.

The great room was as light as the outdoors had been. He had expected a momentary adjustment, going from the bright sunlight to the dim interior, but the Fazi seemed to calibrate their interior light to match their sun's rays. How typical. The light came from the ceiling. Archer glanced up without moving his head, and noted that there were no obvious lighting fixtures. The light coming through a thousand different holes was diffuse and powerful at the same time.

Archer continued walking with purpose, following the instructions he'd been given. He walked straight ahead, into a large chamber, where a dozen Fazi sat in a half circle, each the exact distance from the next.

In this room, the jasmine smell was stronger. Small burners placed on pedestals sent a thin column of smoke into the air. Even with the smoke, the light in here was as strong as it had been everywhere else. There were no shadows in this place, no way for something or someone to hide. Even the smallest expression would be visible.

Up close, the Fazi did not surprise him. Archer had already seen images of them provided by Hoshi and T'Pol. The Fazi were humanoid, like most of the aliens Archer was familiar with. In fact, he would have mistaken them for human if he had seen them first on Earth.

There were only a few differences. All of the Fazi facing him had coarse white hair and sideburns.

They were also shorter than humans. The tallest Fazi never exceeded five feet six inches tall.

He probably looked like a giant to them.

The Fazi did not acknowledge him. If they were surprised at his appearance or the appearance of his crew, they gave no sign. They simply watched as Archer found the spot on the floor that Hoshi had told him to go to.

The polished stone floor was painted in half circles, shrinking smaller and smaller to a dot away from the council bench. Archer stopped exactly on the center spot of the large room.

Behind him his people stopped at the exact same moment, as if they had practiced the move. Then they all bowed as he remained standing straight. So far so good.

Directly in front of him, one of the Fazi councilmen stood. "I am Councilman Draa."

The Fazi spoke in his own language. The translator held by Hoshi translated his words.

The councilman did not even break sentence at the words coming from the translator. "I represent the Fazi High Council and the Fazi people."

"I am Captain Jonathan Archer of the *Starship Enterprise*. I represent the people of the planet Earth."

Archer waited now for the Fazi Draa to speak. Hoshi warned him a number of times to only speak in the same length of sentences and on the same topics as the councilman addressed. But what those topics might be, Hoshi had had no idea.

"This is an historic day," Councilman Draa said, "for the Fazi people."

"It is also an historic day for the people of Earth," Archer said. He felt constrained by this structure. He wanted to talk with them, not parrot their words.

But he didn't want to scare them either. Maybe, over time, they'd get used to human impulsiveness.

After Archer spoke, Councilman Draa sat down.

The silence in the large council chamber seemed to grow with every second. Archer had no idea what he was supposed to do next. And he didn't dare turn around and ask Hoshi's opinion. So he simply stood there, facing the council, keeping his head up and his body still.

All of the Fazi councilmen stared at him.

The seconds ticked past.

The silence in the chamber unnerved him more than the silence outside had. He couldn't even hear the sound of anyone else breathing. Did this place somehow muffle noise? He could hear his own ragged breath, and he suspected everyone else could hear his pounding heart.

Why didn't anyone speak?

Weren't they curious?

Didn't they want to know about the aliens in front of them?

Didn't they want to know about Earth or the starship?

Why didn't they ask what he was doing here?

Maybe their lack of curiosity explained their lack of art, music, and identifiable culture. Maybe it even explained the lack of evidence of war.

He wanted to pace. It took all of his strength to remain still. He hadn't realized what a restless person he was until he was faced with these precise, immobile beings, who seemed so content with silence and inaction.

The Fazi weren't even looking at him. At least not directly. They seemed to be staring beyond his team at the open doors. The jasmine-scented smoke continued to rise, but it was the only thing that moved in the entire room.

For some reason he had expected more. He had never expected silence, and neither had Hoshi or T'Pol, or they would have warned him.

Did he dare speak?

Did he dare turn and walk away?

Which would be the worst sin? He had no idea, and now he understood why both T'Pol and Hoshi wanted him to study these people more. These were very weird folk.

Archer stood there staring straight ahead. The Fazi council sat staring back, their dark eyes and light faces framed by their white hair and sideburns. It was as if a dozen short statues were staring at him. Didn't they even blink?

Archer could feel a drop of sweat starting to ease down the side of his forehead. The old saying about never letting them see you sweat popped into his mind, but he didn't dare move to brush away the drop.

Seconds more ticked past, becoming an eternity.

Maybe they were now waiting for him to say something, to explain why they were there, the reason for this visit. He was the one, after all, who had said he was coming here, and when.

Every moment seemed to stretch.

This was agony. He knew he had to do something and do it quickly. Either speak or turn away.

Turning away would accomplish nothing as far as he was concerned. He was here to make contact with this race, to possibly form a future alliance. And that wasn't going to be done by walking away.

He took a shallow breath, gathered himself and broke the silence. "Councilman Draa, High Council of the Fazi people, the people of Earth have—"

Wrong choice.

As if pulled by the same string, all the councilmen rose, turned their backs on Archer, and disappeared into doors behind their chairs before the last word he had spoken died into the high ceiling.

"Nice meeting you," Archer said as the doors behind every chair clicked shut.

He turned around. Hoshi's face was as white as a sheet and Trip was doing everything in his power to hold back a grin. Reed and Mayweather both looked stunned.

"I think that went well," Archer said, heading between them and toward the big door leading back to the shuttlepod.

Trip snorted.

Reed made a choking sound.

Archer doubted Hoshi was breathing.

Outside he headed across the open and very empty plaza, his people in the same formation behind him. The sun was warm on his face, the breeze light and gentle, and the air felt wonderful.

"Nice day for a walk," he said, just loud enough for Trip to hear beside him.

"I wonder what they'd do," Trip said, his voice just loud enough for Archer to understand, "if we went for a stroll around the plaza, looking at the architecture."

"I think I've already done enough damage," Archer said.

"Yeah," Trip said, clearly barely containing his laughter. "But it was a great speech."

TEN

EXCEPT FOR A FEW LOW-KEY JOKES, NO ONE SAID MUCH AS they came back through the decontamination process and headed for the bridge. There, T'Pol looked up from the navigation table when they entered. She had an expression of disapproval on her face. Archer had expected it. He just hadn't expected to agree with her.

He had purposely not brought her to the meeting with the Fazi. He had wanted this to be an Earth-based first contact, not a Vulcan one. But she had watched everything through the vid-cam recordings of the proceedings, just like they had agreed.

Apparently she now thought even less of him than she had before.

He squared his shoulders and passed between the railings, down the single step to his captain's chair. He didn't sit, however. The restlessness he had felt on the planet had grown.

Meeting another species should have been easy. After a few nods to cultural differences, the goals should have been the same. *Hello. How are you. I'll tell you about my culture if you tell me about yours.* Simple as that. A few questions, a few answers, and then the discussion would be under way.

Or not.

He'd read about the first contact between the Vulcans and the humans. Even factoring in the Vulcans' native reserve, the first contact had gone like that. Some superficial discussion, a mild disagreement about music and food, and then some give-and-take. The give-and-take ended pretty early in the proceedings, of course, since the Vulcans believed that an inferior race shouldn't share their knowledge, but in the beginning it must have been glorious.

Inferior race. Well, he'd helped with that stereotype again, hadn't he?

Archer put a hand on the cool leather back of his chair and watched the rest of his team rejoin the bridge. Everyone seemed subdued and no one met T'Pol's cool gaze. They all felt the mission had failed, just as he did. So, he supposed, it was time to get those feelings into the open.

"Someone want to explain to me what happened down there?" Archer asked.

"You insulted the Fazi High Council," T'Pol said. Of course she spoke first. She hadn't even been down there and she was offering her opinion. She hadn't heard that awful silence or smelled that strange jasmine. Even though the air on *Enterprise* was bottled, Archer was happy to breathe it again. In some ways, it felt like home, a concept he doubted T'Pol understood.

"Yeah," Archer said. "I got that much. Kinda hard to miss when a group of aliens turns their backs to you."

He hadn't meant the sarcasm to be so pronounced, but he had to keep control of this discussion. These were his people. He could communicate with them.

He hoped.

"What I'm trying to figure out," he said, "is exactly what I did to insult them."

"You spoke out of turn," Hoshi said. She had folded one hand over the other and was watching him from her station. The tension he had noted on the planet was gone; apparently, she had expected the worst and it had happened.

Archer felt a surge of anger and he suppressed it. He wasn't angry at his crew. He was angry at his own impatience. They had warned him to wait, and he hadn't. His actions had blown this first contact, not theirs, and they didn't deserve to be punished for his mistake.

"What was I supposed to do?" he asked. "No one said anything else, so I couldn't respond. And it would have been rude to turn around and walk away."

"In our culture, yes," Hoshi said. "In theirs, leaving would have been better."

T'Pol nodded slightly.

"Why?" The frustration in his voice was clear, even to his own ears.

"The meeting was over," Hoshi said.

"Not for me it wasn't," Archer said. "There was a great deal I wanted to talk about."

"Apparently, they didn't want to talk," Hoshi said.

"They probably lack a protocol for dealing with outsiders. They greeted you, then expected you to leave."

"Without asking any questions? Without learning about us?"

"How does a society that structured learn?" Reed asked. The question might have been rhetorical.

Archer frowned at him.

Reed shrugged. "They have dictates for everything. I presume they would also have dictates for learning. Protocols, procedures. A certain rhythm to the way that things are done."

"And I'm supposed to just know this?" Archer asked.

Hoshi sighed. "I should have guessed it. I mean it was right there before us."

"We needed more study," T'Pol said.

"If the culture has so much structure that they haven't even figured out how to deal with outsiders," Archer said, "no amount of study in the world is going to tell us that."

"After time," T'Pol said, "we would realize those protocols were missing."

"We would?" Archer said. "How much time?"

"Study like this can take years," T'Pol said.

"If we spent years on one planet," Archer said, "we'd be wasting our time."

"I disagree," T'Pol said. "Caution is always preferable to haste."

He stared at her. She tilted her head, her dark eyes cool. Her cap of brown hair hadn't moved when her head had, but the new position made her pointed ears more prominent. The superficial differences between humans and Vulcans were slight as well, masking the truly deep disagreements they had about the way they viewed the universe—and themselves.

"You value caution too much," Archer said.

"And your haste is what got you into this situation," T'Pol said.

Archer turned away from her, looking instead at Hoshi. "Okay. We've already established that the Fazi had put me between the proverbial rock and hard place. We don't know if they would have been insulted if we left before they did either."

"Not for a fact, no," Hoshi said. "But a lot of their rules center around speech. Action seems prescribed as well, but not to the same extent. Before we left, I mentioned the rules of the High Council. They were clear. No one could speak out of turn."

"But they can leave out of turn," Archer said, his head spinning.

"I don't believe that leaving was out of turn," Hoshi said. "If this had been a normal away situation, I could have told you that."

"But, because we were following Fazi rules, you couldn't speak up," Archer said.

"Right," Hoshi said.

He spread out his right hand. "Rock." Then he spread out his left. "Hard place."

"More study—" T'Pol started.

"T'Pol." Archer made his voice sting with command. "You're coming dangerously close to violating a rule of the bridge. Don't nag the captain."

"I hadn't been informed of that rule," T'Pol said with great dignity.

Archer grinned at her. "See my dilemma? And how long have you Vulcans been studying humans?"

Her eyes narrowed. He had gotten to her. That pleased him on a small, petty level.

"The insult," Hoshi said, ignoring Archer's interaction with T'Pol, "was not in your words, but in the act of speaking itself. Since it was out of turn, the Fazi had no choice but to leave as they did."

"How do these people get anything done?" Archer asked, forcing himself to take a deep breath and calm down.

"By the book, it would seem," Trip said. "And if it's not in the book, you have to wait until it is."

"Exactly," Hoshi said. "A society of complete control, both in structure and language."

Archer sighed. Then he glanced at the screen. The planet looked so innocuous, so familiar. The way that the Fazi faces had looked familiar. The way that Vulcan faces looked familiar.

"Okay," he said. "Tell me this. Did I do all right with the greeting?"

Hoshi smiled. "You did fine, Captain."

"So there is some hope," he said, circling around his chair. After a moment he sat in it, then stared at the planet again. Maybe this was more important to him than it was to the Fazi. Maybe they didn't care about visitors from the sky. Maybe they lacked curiosity in the way that Vulcans lacked emotion. Maybe they had buried their own curiosity so deep they couldn't even access it anymore.

No one answered his hope remark. He'd expected

T'Pol to disagree. Maybe she was afraid she'd stepped over a protocol she didn't understand.

Archer suppressed a smile. His mood was improving. He leaned back in his chair. "All right. How do I take my foot out of my mouth with these people?"

"Give me another day and I might be able to tell you," Hoshi said. "With T'Pol's help."

Archer glanced at the Vulcan subcommander.

Her level gaze met his. "You already know my opinion on continued study," she said.

"I believe I do," Archer said, letting a bit of that smile out. "One more day."

She gave him a nod that was nearly a bow. From his position near the lift, Trip grinned. He seemed to like T'Pol's discomfort as much as Archer did.

"But this time," Archer said, "I want to be included every step of the way. I don't think I can handle another silence like the one with the High Council again."

"Like a bad date, huh, Captain?" Trip said.

Mayweather made a strangled noise that sounded suspiciously like a suppressed laugh.

"I wouldn't know," Archer said. "Is it?"

Mayweather leaned forward, his shoulders shaking. T'Pol watched them in silence.

Reed wasn't paying attention at all. He was frowning at the screen near his station. "Captain?"

"Yes, Lieutenant?"

"With your permission," Reed said, "I would like to continue to investigate the race living on the southern continent. Something about them doesn't quite make sense."

No one had mentioned the race on the southern continent. Archer wasn't even certain the rest of his crew was looking at them. He frowned at Reed.

"A hunch, Lieutenant?"

"More like an anomaly," Reed said. "It feels like I've seen something that doesn't quite figure, but I can't pinpoint it."

"There's a ton of stuff about this planet that is plain weird," Trip said. "Just add it to the pile."

But Archer wasn't ready to dismiss his security chief's hunches that quickly. One of the reasons Archer was glad to have Reed on board was Reed's ability to assess a situation and make a rapid judgment about it. If he couldn't yet articulate that judgment, fine. He would research it until he could.

Or until something went wrong.

Considering how the first contact had gone, Archer would rather have the research find the so-called anomaly.

"Go ahead," he said.

"I require some better pictures than we can get from orbit," Reed said. "Do I have your permission to fly the shuttlepod in to obtain them?"

"I would advise strongly against any landing," T'Pol said; then she glanced at Archer to see if she had spoken out of turn.

A nervous Vulcan. What a concept. He knew better than to point it out to her.

"I agree," Archer said. "Low flights only. I want to be kept informed on what you discover with them as well. Something about this planet is going to make sense before we leave here."

"Thank you, sir," Reed said.

Archer nodded absently. He was no longer thinking about the southern continent. He was thinking about the first contact. If it took another day or another week, establishing some sort of contact with the Fazi would be worthwhile to Earth. Or maybe just to him. Leaving things as they were was not acceptable.

Captain's log.

Dealing with the Fazi has gotten me to think about protocol, a word I have never liked. T'Pol told me when this began that we needed to establish a protocol for first contacts. Part of me agrees.

If we'd had a protocol, I might not have rushed into first contact with the Fazi. I must admit that Ensign Hoshi and Subcommander T'Pol warned me about moving too quickly, and I did not heed their warnings. I am hoping that my mistake of speaking out of turn with the Fazi will be correctable, as soon as we discover how to do so. But I can see that dealing with this culture is going to be as frustrating at times as dealing with the Vulcans.

But I'm not sure how much a protocol would have helped. The Fazi's protocols prevented them from interacting with us at all. If we're too regulated, we might miss the adventure. I can't permit that.

Perhaps guidelines might be the answer—

suggestions without the sting of regulation. I'll talk to T'Pol about the subject later.

On another, related topic, I have also been considering what might happen when we do establish relations with the Fazi. At that point, how much should I tell them about the greater universe beyond their system? And what technology, if any, should I share with them? On this topic I know how the Vulcans feel. And I know how I feel about how the Vulcans held Earth back for so long.

But I worry that the Fazi, with their strict regulations and their need for structure, might find all this information disruptive. I certainly don't want to be the one to damage their native culture.

Everything about first contact seemed so clear when we left Earth. Now nothing does.

ELEVEN

FOR THE SECOND NIGHT IN A ROW, CUTLER HAD FOR-
gone her Vulcan broth. This time, she'd eaten the veg-
etable salad the chef had made to go with the stew.
The stew did smell better than it had a few days before and she had been tempted, but she hadn't eaten
any. Visions of microbes still danced in her brain.

Visions of the failed Fazi first contact danced in
everyone else's. Mayweather had described what he'd
seen to everyone who had asked. Now he seemed
tired of it. Or maybe the entire experience had been
so discouraging he didn't want to discuss it anymore.

He had been the one to suggest continuing the
game. Cutler had thought no one would want to
play after the day's events. After all, there was a real-
life adventure going on around them. But the captain
had ordered more study, and no one was going back
to the planet for a while.

Diversion, Mayweather had said, was just what
they needed.

The mess hall still had a dozen or so crewmen in it as Cutler spread out the towel she had brought to cushion the sound of the bolts on the hard tabletop. Novakovich had brought fresh coffee for everyone at the gaming table, and as he set it down, he grinned.

"Expecting a long night, crewman?" Cutler asked.

"Expecting to find part of a Universal Translator, sir!" he said crisply.

She raised her eyebrows in amusement. "We'll just have to see about that."

She took her coffee cup and set it on the table behind her. The last thing she wanted was to spill on the bolts. The red dye she used might be water soluble. She hadn't checked.

"Everyone remember where we left off?" she asked.

Mayweather nodded, holding up a painted bolt. "You know we could figure out a way to put dice together."

"The bolts are working fine," Anderson said. "I like the weight of them in the cup before it gets dumped."

"Weight?" Novakovich asked. "Why? Does it make the decision seem important?"

"Naw," Anderson said. "It just serves to remind me that we're always down to the nuts and bolts in this game."

"How come you didn't use nuts?" Novakovich asked.

"Trip didn't have any to spare, but these short, stubby bolts were in great supply."

"I can make you a die or two," Mayweather said. "Or rather, Trip can."

"I'm sure Trip has better things to do," Cutler said.

"I probably could have made dice too, but getting the sides even and making sure they rolled properly seemed too fussy for this game."

"Are you saying we're doing this on the fly?" Anderson asked, a twinkle in his eye.

"Of course we are," she said. "If we were doing it properly, we'd be on the computer, linked up from our quarters—and following preset rules."

"How come no one thought to put an RPG in the ship's files?" Novakovich asked.

"Gee," Mayweather said. "Maybe they thought about putting in files that might be useful instead of fun."

"No ship would ever waste space on recreation," Anderson said. "If it did, then the mess would be bigger and more comfortable. I think this one's actually designed to get people out of here quickly."

"It probably is," Cutler said, setting the bolt cup on the table. "Do you all remember where we are?"

"We're in the mess," Novakovich said, scratching at his face.

Anderson grabbed his wrist. "Let's not," he said with a shudder.

Novakovich grinned. "Sorry. I forgot."

Anderson swallowed, looking a little green. Apparently the transporter accident Novakovich had suffered made Anderson nervous.

It made them all nervous.

"In the game," Anderson said, leaning forward, "we're on the second floor of a building."

"Hiding after we blew away a bunch of Martians," Mayweather said.

"Expecting more to return," Novakovich said.

"So what options do we have?" Anderson asked.

Cutler glanced at her notes. "You can go back down the ramp, or up the ramp to the next floor. There are sky bridges to three other buildings five floors above you."

"And I assume some problems," Anderson said.

"That's the point of this game," Mayweather said. "Fight through the problems and get the rewards."

"I say we go up," Novakovich said. "Figure out where to go when we reach the sky bridges."

Both Anderson and Mayweather agreed, so Cutler glanced at her notes. "There's a slight chance of a Martian nest on the third floor."

She took the cup of bolts and dumped it out on the towel. The noise of the bolts on the table was still loud enough to draw the attention of a few of the remaining diners nearby.

"Four red," she said. "The floor is clear."

"Up to the fourth," Mayweather said.

She dumped out the bolts again. "Five red," she said. "Fourth floor's clear."

"One more to go until we hit the sky bridge level," Anderson said.

She dumped out the bolts for the third time. Her notes had it that for each floor they attempted, the chance of a Martian nest went up. Two or less for the second floor, three or less for the third, four or less for the fourth. When she dumped the bolts this time, there were seven red.

They all looked at her as she smiled. "Still safe."

"So what are we looking at?" Anderson asked.

Cutler smiled and called up a file on her padd. In

that file, she had drawn the map of the center area of the Martian city. Each box was city block, and she had drawn lines between the boxes where there was a sky bridge.

She set the padd in the middle of the table, keeping her hand on it so no one called up her gaming notes.

"The piece of the Universal Translator is in the basement of this building," she said, pointing to a four-block-large building in the center of the map. Then she pointed to a building near the edge of the city. "You are here, on the fifth floor."

"Wow, you've really put some work into this," Mayweather said.

"I had to," Cutler said, "to stay ahead of you three."

Novakovich laughed. "And to make sure she made up the rules before we questioned her on them. Right?"

"Exactly," Cutler said. "Someone has to establish what is going on, and since I built this world, I get to be the one that does it."

"Don't you wish it was that easy in real life?" Anderson asked, staring at the map.

"Sometimes it is," Cutler said.

"I don't think so," Mayweather said, all amusement gone from his face. "Captain Archer is making up the rules as he goes along, and I'll bet he didn't think today was easy."

"I didn't say it was always easy," Cutler said. She didn't envy the captain. She was glad to be a mere ensign, working on her science projects. "I can't imagine his job ever is."

"Why's that?" Anderson asked.

"Being that we are the first Earth starship out here," Cutler said, "I think he is forced to make up the rules. In much the same fashion that I made up the rules to this game. I had a basic idea how it was supposed to work and we've been winging it ever since."

"That sounds exactly right," Mayweather said.

Novakovich shook his head. "At least Captain Archer isn't running into Martians with pointed teeth and sharp knives."

"After seeing the Fazi High Council," Mayweather said, "I'd bet the captain would love a nasty green Martian."

"Sharp little pointy teeth sound like they're easier to deal with than someone else's rules," Novakovich said.

Anderson looked at Cutler. "I'm not so sure," Anderson said. "I have a feeling we might regret having this conversation."

Cutler just smiled. "Shall we continue?" she asked.

TWELVE

ARCHER STOOD AT THE SCIENCE STATION BESIDE HIS chief of security, Lieutenant Reed, and stared at the screen before him. T'Pol sat in front of them, manipulating the images. She had already seen them.

The rest of the bridge crew worked at their stations. Hoshi had her earpieces on and seemed to be listening intently. Trip had brought her food twice and had tried to talk her into going to her quarters to rest, but she had refused. She wanted to get as many answers as she could in the time Archer had given her.

Archer was beginning to get the sense that the rest of the crew thought the twenty-four-hour window was too short. But as he had said to T'Pol, he wasn't going to orbit this planet forever. There were other planets to discover, other places to see. He just wanted to make this first contact right before moving on.

It hadn't seemed like a lot to ask.

He focused on the images before him. Reed had taken the shuttlepod over the southern continent immediately after Archer had given him permission. He had already analyzed the images, then had shown them to T'Pol. Now they were sharing the information with Archer.

When he had said he wanted to be included in the loop, he hadn't meant that the crew would loop around him last. He'd tell them that, after they finished looking at the southern continent.

He could see why it had disturbed Reed. Even from afar, the primitive look of the structures felt deceptive—almost like a primitive village designed for tourists. But he hadn't been able to put his finger on why the villages disturbed him either, not until he'd seen Reed's low-flying imagery.

"The building construction is much more sophisticated than we had first thought," Reed said. "It is far above any primitive level."

He pointed to three different areas on the continent. Archer pushed a few buttons himself to bring one of the images in closer. The building he was looking at seemed simple enough—a hut with a single door. But unlike most primitive dwellings, where the marks of construction were clear, he couldn't tell how this building had been put together or even how long ago.

Simple and sophisticated. It sent a shiver down his back and he didn't know why.

"How far above primitive is it?" Archer asked. Architecture was not his strong suit.

"I'd say a great deal above." Reed glanced at T'Pol for confirmation.

"This is the design and architecture of an older race, not a primitive one," she said.

"Were there any signals when you flew over?" Archer asked. "Did they try to contact you?"

"There wasn't even a sign that they cared." Reed crossed his arms and frowned. "Here's the thing: On the surface I found no energy signatures at all. However, when I altered our scanners to look for underground energy sources, here's what I found."

He brought up another image. It showed no sign of energy being used on land, or under the land, but offshore, under the water, there was a lot. Along a small area of coastline, there were so many indications of energy signatures coming from under the water, it looked like a city lit up at night.

Archer peered at the image. In its own way, it was beautiful. He touched a finger to the screen as if he were checking to see if the image would vanish. It didn't, of course.

"There's no mistake?" Archer said. "This wasn't the result of faulty equipment?"

"No," Reed said. "I double- and triple-checked. When I scanned for large energy signatures of the type typically found underground—"

"In Earth cultures," T'Pol added, mostly to herself.

"—I got these readings. Now look at this. This one's even more interesting."

Reed pulled the image back to show the energy signatures around the entire continent. "We took this from low orbit," he said.

It was as if the landmass were surrounded by a halo. "Amazing," Archer said. "What do you make of all this?"

"If these readings are accurate," T'Pol said, "and

since we have no reason to doubt them, we must assume they are, then we can reliably state that the culture on the southern continent is a predominantly water-based civilization that is quite advanced. It may be as advanced as the Fazi."

"From what I can tell," Reed said, "they show no interest in building anything for mobility. I saw no vehicles, no carts. The roads appear to be designed for walking only."

"On land," T'Pol said.

"None of the energy signatures we gathered from under water were moving either."

T'Pol nodded.

Archer stared at the low-orbit image of the southern continent showing energy readings surrounding it. He found this fascinating, even more fascinating than the Fazi.

The Fazi, if truth be told, unnerved him a little. He disliked their fanatical adherence to structure and organization. He frowned slightly. He hadn't been willing to think about his discomfort with the Fazi until now, until the *Enterprise* had discovered a puzzle in the southern continent.

Had the Vulcans been this uncomfortable when they'd come to Earth? It was clear that the Vulcans disapproved of many human traits, much in the same way Archer disapproved of the Fazi need for structure. Was this part of first contact as well, learning to step over your own likes and dislikes to see a culture for what it was, not what you wanted it to be?

"Captain?" Reed asked.

Archer had been so lost in thought he wasn't sure what Reed was asking him. "Hmm?" he said.

"I asked if it makes a difference that this culture is more advanced than we originally suspected."

Good question. Archer didn't have an answer for it. As if he didn't have enough trouble with trying to figure out how to communicate with the Fazi, now he had another race to interact with.

"It makes a difference," Archer said, "although I'm not sure exactly what kind of difference it makes."

Water-based culture. How difficult would that be to communicate with? He turned toward Hoshi, but she was still absorbed in her work with the Fazi language.

He sighed. He didn't want to interrupt her, at least not yet.

"So now what do you suggest?" Archer asked Reed and T'Pol.

"Do not try to contact them," T'Pol said.

"I agree," Reed said. "Allow me to do more study and I'll see what I can find out."

Archer nodded, then glanced at Hoshi again. She hadn't even noticed the work going on at the science station. He wondered if she was even aware of the bridge at all.

"I wouldn't know how to even go about contacting them," Archer said to Reed. "Do you?"

"I have no idea whatsoever, sir," Reed said.

T'Pol said nothing. Archer wondered if she had an idea—if Vulcans had contacted water-based civilizations before—but he didn't ask. She'd volunteer the information if she had to.

"Well, keep investigating in any way you can next to trying to talk to one of them. And be cautious."

"Yes, sir," Reed said.

T'Pol raised a single eyebrow as she looked at Archer. He could have sworn he surprised her. He even surprised himself. Be cautious. Where had that come from?

Where had any of this come from? Going slow, taking his time, studying his options, had never been a strength of his. From the looks of how the exploration of this planet was going, he had better learn how to do it.

Although he didn't have to like it.

THIRTEEN

ONCE AGAIN, THE GAME HAD BECOME HER WORLD. Ruined buildings, green Martian hordes, and her favorite—the flying Martian lizards—were all there waiting, waiting for her players to stumble onto them. Waiting to challenge the entire group.

The three men had been studying the map of the ancient city for at least an hour, discussing their options, asking her sideways questions that she wasn't answering, shaking their heads. At one point, each player had gotten up, circled the table, hands behind his back, like those ancient generals she'd studied in school. Then they would sit back down and argue a bit more.

Of course, they were now the only people in the mess. Everyone else had left. She would have thought that she would force them to play by reminding them that Mayweather's Unk character was nominally their leader, judging by his charisma score, but she didn't. She found the arguments as fascinating as the game.

However, if the men took much longer she was going to have a horde of Martians come into the building below and force them into a decision. But she didn't tell them that.

"Let's take the right sky bridge." Anderson drew his finger along what he thought would be the best route to the prize. "This way we only have to cross five sky bridges."

"I didn't even see that," Novakovich said, "and I thought I'd studied the map from all angles."

Cutler thought he had too—and some of them were angles she hadn't even thought of.

"All right," Mayweather said. He picked up the supply and weapons list she had made for them. "We have rope. Let's tie ourselves together for this first crossing, just in case this sky bridge has rotted out."

Cutler hid her surprise. Mayweather was ahead of her again. There were rotted sky bridges in this city, although this wasn't one of them.

Mayweather looked at her and smiled, but she kept her face as blank as she could. She was getting better at hiding information from them. Thank heavens. She thought the first part of the game had been too easy, partly because the players had read the answers to their questions on her face.

"Okay, we're tied," Novakovich said. "Mayweather, I think Unk should go first, since he's the weakest. That way Rust and Dr. Mean are here to pull him up."

"Got it," Mayweather said. "Setting out across the bridge."

Cutler picked up the cup of bolts and handed it to Mayweather. "Let's see if Unk gets across."

Mayweather dumped out the cup onto the towel, four red bolts up.

"He made it," Cutler said. She didn't tell them that to make it all he had to do was show anything better than two red bolts on this first bridge. That number would go up as they crossed more bridges.

Anderson's Dr. Mean followed and made it safely with six red bolts. Novakovich's Rust brought up the rear, also safely, with three red bolts.

"So which way next?" Cutler asked. "You have two sky bridges or you could go up or down inside the building."

"Since we're still tied together," Anderson said, "let's head across another sky bridge, see if we can get closer to the center of this city."

The other two agreed and they repeated the process. This time Cutler knew they had to have four or more red bolts to make it safely. All three did.

"The sky bridges in this building are two floors in either direction." Cutler pointed at the map. "The one headed toward the center is two floors up. The other two are down."

"Up," Novakovich said.

"We're trapping ourselves higher in a tall building," Mayweather said. "Are we sure we want to do that?"

"Are there any signs of Martians living in this building?" Anderson asked.

Cutler shook her head. "No Martian nests within two floors, however, most of the windows have been broken out, and there are signs of large birds living here. Most people call them flying lizards because of their long, sharp claws and scales on their tails."

She barely hid her delight. She'd worked hard on the flying lizards. She'd be happy when they got into play.

"How large are they?" Mayweather asked.

"Large enough to use a Martian as a midnight snack," Cutler said. "Ugly green Martian is one of their favorite foods."

"I still say we go up," Novakovich said.

"Man, you're a glutton for punishment," Mayweather said, but he didn't disagree with Novakovich's decision.

"Okay, we're untied," Anderson said. "Let's do it."

Cutler shook the cup of bolts and tipped it out onto the towel. Six red. "No problem making it to the next sky bridge."

"Okay, let's get tied back up," Anderson said.

"This sky bridge has piles of garbage in places across from it," Cutler said. "And most of the windows are broken out. The Martian wind is pretty strong and you can see some of the flying lizards circling in the distance on updrafts."

"Can we stop and enjoy the view?" Anderson asked. "It sounds like something I'd want to look at."

"You have a real death wish," Novakovich said.

Mayweather was ignoring them. "Is it clear from where we stand that they use this bridge as a perch?"

Good question. Cutler was becoming more and more convinced that if she ever got into trouble again on an away mission, she hoped it was with

Mayweather. He seemed to be an extremely clear thinker. She hadn't realized that before.

"Yes," she said. "They use the bridge as a perch."

Novakovich shuddered. He started to pick at the sand pimples on this face, and then stopped.

"But are there any flying lizards on the bridge now?" Anderson asked.

"No, there are not."

"How about we take a break right here?" Novakovich said. "I have a feeling this bridge isn't going to be as easy as the last two, and I need some sleep."

Cutler glanced around the mess hall. Again they were the only four from their shift left, and the lights in the other half of the room had been dimmed.

She wondered who had done that, and when. She really did lose track of time when she was playing, just as she had as a kid on the computer. In some ways, she preferred playing this way. It felt less contrived somehow, almost like pure imagination. It was as if this group, through the power of their minds, had created a whole new world.

"Good idea," Mayweather said. "I have duty on the bridge when Captain Archer tries to contact the Fazi again. I don't want to miss that."

Cutler smiled. "You think the Fazi are more interesting than flying Martian lizards?"

Mayweather's eyes twinkled. "How am I supposed to answer that? If I say yes, I insult you and the game."

"I think seeing a real Martian flying lizard, when we've been told they don't exist, would be a lot more exciting than seeing Fazi," Anderson said.

"You haven't seen Fazi," Mayweather said.

"Not yet." Anderson collected the bolts. "But I hope to someday."

"Do you hope to see a Martian flying lizard?" Novakovich asked.

"Only in the game," Anderson said. "Only in the game."

FOURTEEN

Captain's log.

We have discovered that there are two fairly advanced races inhabiting this planet. The humanoid Fazi are so similar to us that we had no trouble figuring out what stage of development they're in. We almost missed the other race. If it weren't for Lieutenant Reed, we would have.

We have no name for the other species yet. It's crab- or spiderlike, and it does most of its living underwater, which presents interesting problems of its own.

I thought the Fazi were difficult to understand. I'm very worried about a water-based culture. We may have even less in common with it than with the Fazi.

The other thing that concerns me is how these two races developed. My science team tells me that independent development of two such vastly different races is very un-usual. Apparently, it's quite common to have different races on a planet—and even differ-ent sentient races—but it's very unusual that more than one race would become advanced independently of the other.

Usually, if more than one race evolves, it has contact with the other races and they evolve too—or they destroy each other in a war.

T'Pol has confirmed the science team's find-ings. She also volunteered some information of her own, which surprised me. She's done very little volunteering on this mission, and what she has volunteered has mostly been words of caution, words I haven't heeded.

She says she has only heard of two other planets where two cultures, so vastly differ-ent, evolved. And one always destroyed the other before they reached spaceflight capa-bilities. Considering Earth's history, I can un-derstand that. Yet here the Fazi are far from warlike, and the two races do not even have a common border.

Each must know that the other exists, but I can't even be certain of that. The Fazi's need for structure may have kept them away from the oceans and from discovering the other race. Although that doesn't entirely make sense to me either. Why not explore your own planet first before turning to outer space?

Of course, there I go again, making as-

*sumptions based on my own experience. But
how else does a person understand his envi-
ronment? And what is experience for if it
doesn't inform the decisions you make down
the road?*

*I am usually not this contemplative. I much
prefer to take action first and suffer the consequences later. I'm beginning to think that if
the only way to have contact with alien races
is to study, study, study, and then tentatively
open dialogues, I'm the wrong guy for the job.*

*In an hour we're going to try to contact the
Fazi again and if they will listen I will apologize for my gaffe in protocol. If somehow we
can set up a dialogue with them, I hope to
ask them about the race on the southern
continent. Maybe then we can start figuring
out how this place works.*

ARCHER PACED FASTER THAN USUAL AROUND HIS
captain's chair. Once the dialogue with the Fazi
began, he wouldn't be able to move. He was trying
to get all of his nervous tics out of the way now, so
that they wouldn't tempt him later.

The crew was trying to ignore him, all except
T'Pol, who had a slight frown, as if she were worried
that he had somehow lost his mind. Maybe he had.
He was so wrapped up in trying to figure out what
to say when that he felt like a kid about to ask the
very first girl he was attracted to—ever—on a first
date. He'd blushed and stammered back then. He
was afraid he'd do the same thing now.

It wasn't a first date, dammit (and damn Trip for giving him that idea in the first place). It was a first contact—well, a second contact really, and he was going to do it right this time.

Trip was on the bridge in his usual spot near the lift, watching Archer with amusement. These last few days, Archer felt as if he'd been placed on the ship solely to amuse Trip. At least that was working.

Hoshi was finishing her preparations on the translator. Reed was monitoring all of the communications for other security problems. Mayweather was keeping an eye on the orbit as well as the dark screen ahead. He seemed preoccupied by something, but when Archer had asked him what it was, Mayweather had mumbled something about Martian flying lizards and then refused to elaborate.

"You have thirty seconds, Captain," Reed said, as if Archer didn't know that.

"Relax, sir," Hoshi said, even though she was far from the picture of calmness. "I have the translator programmed so that no matter what you say, it will come out in the correct grammatical fashion for the Fazi."

"Great." Archer stopped and faced the screen. He shook the tension from his arms, then squared his shoulders. *Do not move,* he reminded himself.

"Just remember not to speak until it is your turn," Hoshi said.

"That's not going to be easy," Trip said.

Archer turned and gave him a dirty look, which only made Trip chuckle.

"Three seconds, sir," Reed said.

Archer faced the screen again just as the image of

Councilman Draa appeared. Draa was standing in front of a black cloth that outlined his skull and made his white hair shine with a light of its own.

Hoshi had told Archer that he would speak first, as was custom, since he had asked for this second audience. It had taken her a while to find the procedure on this, since apparently, a single audience was customary. Rarely did anyone return for a second.

"Councilman Draa," Archer said, "thank you for allowing me to speak with you again. I apologize for my previous breach of Fazi etiquette. I am new to your culture and beg your forgiveness."

"It is the council who wishes to apologize," Councilman Draa said.

Archer could sense movement around him. His staff was surprised by Draa's admission. Neither T'Pol nor Hoshi had expected it.

But he didn't let their reaction distract him. Archer remained focused on the screen.

Draa was saying, "We should not have held someone alien to us and our culture to our standards."

Archer wasn't sure if that was an insult or not. It probably was. All cultures thought they were superior to other cultures, even if the other culture was more sophisticated. Humans knew that Vulcans were technologically advanced, but thought that Vulcans came up short in the personality department.

Draa said nothing further. Archer waited two beats, making sure that the councilman was finished before he spoke. "It is the hope of the people of the planet Earth that a dialogue may be set up that would benefit both races."

"Your arrival caused us great turmoil," Draa said. "It forced us to change our belief that we were alone in the stars."

"As others arriving on our planet not that long ago changed that same belief with my people," Archer said.

"That is welcome information," the councilman said. "May I ask how many races there are among the stars?"

"I wish I could give you an exact count," Archer said, "but I do not believe anyone, of any race, knows the true answer. My people have met many alien races so far, and we have not ventured very far from home."

"So those of us who have believed the universe is full of life have been correct?"

So there was discussion and debate in the Fazi culture. Archer hadn't been sure, and Hoshi hadn't been able to give him an answer.

"Very much so," Archer said. "We have a member of another race, the Vulcans, with us."

Archer motioned for T'Pol to step forward. She did, her hands clasped together before her. Her movements were economical. She did not move any part of her body above the waist because, she had told Archer before the dialogue began, some cultures used gestures for communication even more than words.

"Greetings," Draa said. Archer wasn't certain, but it seemed like his sideburns had rippled.

T'Pol stayed one step behind Archer and bent slightly at the waist. "Greetings from the Vulcan people, Councilor." With that she stepped back, without turning away, and out of the line of the viewscreen.

Well done, Archer thought. Maybe that was what he should have done at the first meeting.

Draa certainly didn't seem upset about the brevity of T'Pol's greeting. "Your starship must be wondrous to have two races existing in it at the same time."

"It is," Archer said. "But we are just as surprised to learn that there are two races existing on your planet."

"Two races?" the councilor asked. "I do not understand."

Archer glanced back at Hoshi, whose face was white. T'Pol stood motionless, giving him no help either. So he decided to just venture forward. "The race that inhabits your planet's southern continent. They are also very advanced."

The councilor looked for a moment as if Archer had shot him. Archer dared not say anything, so he stood and waited as the head of the Fazi council clearly gasped for breath. Then finally Draa reached forward and cut off the signal.

The image of the councilor's face was replaced by the image of the Fazi world from high orbit.

"You have to be getting tired of chewing on that foot of yours," Trip said.

Archer stared at the screen for a moment, then turned around to face his crew. "So what just happened there?"

"You insulted them again," T'Pol said.

"Because I moved my head?" Archer asked. His entire body ached from being so still. The head movement had happened before he had even thought about it.

Hoshi, her face white, just shrugged. "I can't imagine that a simple movement would create so much trouble."

"It does happen," T'Pol said. "However, he seemed distressed before you moved."

"I thought things were going great," Trip said, "up until you mentioned that other race. Maybe that's like mentioning the other woman to a man's wife."

"Okay, that's it," Archer said. "Before I screw up this first contact for a third time, I want to know everything there is to know about both of these cultures."

"It was what I said should be done from the first," T'Pol said, her voice level and calm.

"I know, I know," Archer said, waving away her justified *I told you so.* "Just do it. And do it quickly. I'm not staying here one minute longer than I have to. Understand?"

The bridge was silent as everyone nodded.

FIFTEEN

MAYWEATHER FLEW THE SHUTTLEPOD THROUGH THE atmosphere, heading toward the alien village on the southern continent. Behind him sat Ensign Elizabeth Cutler and Crewman Jamal Edwards. Cutler had been unusually silent during the flight; Mayweather had gotten used to her guiding missions, not participating in one.

In fact, it felt odd not to have Anderson and Novakovich here, asking questions and determining the course of action. They had become a little team in just playing that silly game, and the camaraderie had spread to real life.

Real life: flying over an alien village in a shuttlepod. Mayweather grinned. Even though he'd grown up in space, he'd never quite imagined himself doing this. How often was real life better than the life you'd imagined for yourself? Not very.

Mayweather took the shuttlepod in low over the alien village, making sure no one was around. From the scans, there weren't any life signs, but before he set down, he wanted a visual.

The village was laid out along the seashore. A rugged beach formed a slight barrier between the buildings and the water. The sea was calm—or so it seemed at the moment. It was also deep. Mayweather could see a drop-off less than fifty meters from the beach, a drop-off that didn't allow him to see the ocean floor.

He maneuvered the shuttlepod over the village proper. The buildings were like nothing he'd ever seen before. Built out of some sort of blue and orange material, they looked like misshapen igloos at first glance. On closer inspection, it was clear they were designed with a flow and pattern that was both alien and beautiful at the same time.

They weren't laid out in the efficient, precise patterns that marked the Fazi cities. These buildings seemed to have been placed randomly and without regard for aesthetics. Some of the entries faced other entries. At other times, the entries faced nothing at all. And not once did the entries face the sea.

The buildings were also different sizes. The smallest buildings were short as well as narrower than the rest. And the large ones were huge.

"Amazing," Edwards said, staring out the window. "Look at that doorway. It has to be fifty paces across."

Cutler nodded. "I've seen similar structures in certain spider nests."

"Oh, that's comforting," Edwards said.

Mayweather read no life signs. That wasn't unexpected. These creatures were water-based life-forms.

T'Pol had hypothesized that they only used the villages at certain times. Apparently this wasn't one of those times.

"All right," Mayweather said, glancing back at Cutler. "No life signs. Where do you want me to set this down?"

Cutler was nominally in charge of this mission, something Mayweather found amusing. She usually didn't run missions, but she was the exobiologist and they were trying to find out more about the aliens, so she got to choose things like landing sites. It just felt as if the tables were turned somewhat—he was asking her what she planned to do next.

"Let's land near the big building just ahead." Cutler was already gathering her sample pack and her scanner. "I should be able to get some pretty decent samples there."

"We could open the door as well," Edwards said. "Maybe take a quick running look inside."

"Make it real quick," Mayweather said. "The captain gave us permission for a touch-and-go. If I'm on the ground for longer than a minute, we're all in trouble."

"We'll be here for fifty seconds tops even if we open a door." Cutler gave Edwards a significant look. Edwards grinned.

"Fifty seconds tops," he said. "I promise."

They'd better do that. Mayweather wasn't going to screw up this away mission. As they went lower, he punched on the cameras outside the shuttlepod.

"Visuals on," he said to the *Enterprise* bridge crew.

"We have it nice and clear, Ensign." Captain Archer's voice sounded strong.

"Coming in," Mayweather said.

He maneuvered the shuttlepod next to the building, hovered for a moment, then touched down. As he did so, he used a lever to pop the door. Immediately a fishy smell filled the shuttlepod. He could see the building's wall, so close that he would have skimmed it if he had landed any closer.

"Go!" he shouted.

Cutler climbed out, moving as fast as she could. Edwards was right behind her. Mayweather sat, keeping the shuttlepod ready for a quick takeoff. This entire mission worried him. And T'Pol's objections to it didn't help. She had insisted it was critical they not be seen, and if any of the aliens came up out of the water, the shuttlepod was to leave at once.

Mayweather could hear the ocean lapping against the shore, a curiously familiar sound on an alien world. He hadn't expected it, any more than he'd expected to smell salty air beneath that fishy odor that had first crept into the shuttlepod.

He watched through the windows as Cutler headed to the side of the large open doorway, her scanner in her hand. Edwards ran toward the door, recording everything as he went.

Mayweather could hear Edwards as if the man were inside the shuttlepod.

"The main pathways are slick with mud," Edwards said, suddenly slowing as he neared the entrance. "They curve, then head toward the ocean."

Cutler was using a small tool to chip at the side of the building. Her hands were shaking. Mayweather glanced at the readout. "Come on," he whispered. "Get moving."

"Got it." Cutler put a small piece of the building material in her sack.

"Thirty seconds," Mayweather said. He couldn't help himself. The longer they were on this rock, the more nervous he became.

"Wow, you ought to see the inside of this," Edwards said. "Beautiful."

"Get the picture and head back," Mayweather ordered. "Now!"

"On my way," Edwards said, but he sounded reluctant. This was, after all, the first time he'd ever set foot on an alien planet. Mayweather knew the excitement. He was also keenly aware of the danger.

Cutler was heading back to the shuttle at full run. Edwards gave the building one last glimpse, then turned, his feet slipping on the mud.

At that moment Mayweather saw the first alien coming up out of the water, not more than a hundred paces away on the beach. The alien was huge, looking like a large black rock as it broke the surface.

"You have company," Mayweather said.

The first alien scrambled up the narrow beach. It had eight legs. Water glistened off its hard back. Mayweather couldn't make out a face, and that creeped him more than anything.

"Get out of there, people." Captain Archer's voice broke in over the shuttlepod's com system.

Cutler didn't need to be told twice. She hit the shuttlepod steps and almost dove inside.

Three more aliens came out of the water, and scrambled up the beach.

Edwards lost his footing, caught himself with a hand against the mud, and then got to his feet. He was still thirty paces away. The alien was closing fast.

"Come on," Mayweather muttered.

The alien stopped for a brief moment in front of the shuttlepod. Mayweather would have guessed that the thing was trying to figure out what the pod was, but he'd been warned against giving aliens human traits.

Not being able to see the thing's face made this even harder.

Edwards was running now. In a few seconds, he'd reach the ship.

Suddenly he screamed and spun around, grabbing at his head as if something were poking at him.

"Edwards is under attack," Mayweather said. "Alien is closing. He will not be able to make it in time."

"Mayweather, get out of there now," Captain Archer ordered.

"I'm not leaving Edwards," Mayweather shouted, yanking out his pistol. He was going to go down there and grab Edwards. Maybe if he was lucky, he'd get Edwards before those creatures got their hairy legs on him.

Cutler had her pistol out as well. She was still standing in the door, getting ready to fire. But she didn't seem clear about what she was firing at. So far, nothing was touching Edwards.

Edwards was spinning in a circle, grabbing at his head. One of the aliens was coming fast, far faster than Edwards could have run, even if he was trying.

"You're leaving now, Ensign," Archer shouted through the com. "That's an order. We're transporting Edwards out."

Mayweather cursed. He hated leaving a man behind and he'd seen what the transporter could do. Novakovich was lucky to be alive, in Mayweather's opinion. But he wasn't going to get close to that stupid beam. It was scarier to him than the aliens approaching Edwards.

"Get away from the door," he said to Cutler, then hit the lift controls.

Cutler grabbed one of the seats. She was screaming something at him, something about Edwards, but he didn't hear it. He got the shuttlepod off the ground without skimming the side of the building. He went over the approaching aliens. They looked even uglier from above.

Dammit, he hated leaving Edwards there.

Alarms warned Mayweather that the door was still open, but he didn't care. He'd put a few klicks between him and those creatures; then he would slow enough to get the hatch closed.

Wind whipped at him as the shuttlepod moved inland, away from the alien village, skimming over the trees and rocks.

Cutler pulled herself into the seat beside him. Her normally neat hair was plastered against her face. She was sweating and pale.

"Edwards was beamed out," she said. She must have seen it. Mayweather missed that part, and he was heartily glad.

"But," Cutler said, "I think they got an alien with him."

Mayweather thought about the transporter alcove. Edwards would arrive in that tiny space with a huge creature beside him. Or around him. No one would be expecting it, and they would all dive for cover.

What would the thing do when it realized it was on the *Enterprise?* What could those things do? He hadn't seen a face or claws. But they had been able to build those incredible structures, so somehow these aliens used tools.

He shuddered. "I'm glad I'm not up there at the moment. I wouldn't want to be the first one to come face-to-face with that giant spider-thing in a small hallway."

"Let's hope there's a ship left up there when we get back," Cutler said. She didn't seem to be kidding. But then, he'd already been introduced to her imagination, filled with Martian flying lizards, collapsing bridges, and ruined cities. Of course she would think the worst.

The shuttlepod whipped slightly with the wind. Cutler pulled strands of hair out of her face. "Would you mind slowing down a little?"

He glared at her.

"I want to close the hatch," she said. "It's windy in here."

Windy. The wind wasn't bothering her and he knew it. The close brush with death was. Death or whatever was going to happen when those huge aliens reached the shuttlepod.

Whatever might have been happening to Edwards.

Mayweather put those thoughts out of his mind. He slowed the shuttlepod, made it hover, and watched as Cutler pulled the hatch closed. She settled in beside him. The interior of the shuttle felt almost normal now.

Almost. He'd never flown it with a complement this small.

"Let's get the hell out of here," he said, and blasted the shuttlepod for orbit.

SIXTEEN

THE MOMENT CAPTAIN ARCHER GAVE THE ORDER FOR THE emergency beam-out, Lieutenant Reed and two of his crew fell into position beside the transporter pad. They had drilled for this—an emergency beam-out triggered by an alien attack—but they'd never experienced it.

He'd been warned that anything could come through that transporter—and he'd seen what "anything" meant when Novakovich came through weeks ago, twigs and debris fused with his body.

But the transporter technology had other inaccuracies as well, and one of the reasons Reed drilled his team for just this moment was something he really didn't want to contemplate.

What if the beam caught the aliens, but not the crewman? What if Edwards was still down there, suffering whatever it was that he'd been suffering when Archer ordered the beam-out?

There was no way to tell. Archer had ordered the shuttlepod to leave.

Reed held his phase pistol tightly, preparing to use it as the beam particles materialized on the pad. Lots of dark matter. Lots of unrecognizable body parts. Hairy black legs that had inverted joints. A black carapace and a human arm.

Reed froze, not wanting to see what was coming next. Man fused with alien, both dead. Everyone knew that was a possibility. No one wanted to deal with it. Not even his team, who shifted uncomfortably from foot to foot.

The beam-in seemed to take forever, even though Reed knew it only took a few seconds. And as it completed, Reed realized that the tangle of arms and black alien legs hadn't happened because the two beings had fused together, but because they had been beamed up side by side, so close that they seemed tangled.

His relief vanished almost as quickly as it appeared. The alien was huge, spiderlike, and strong. Edwards wasn't small and the creature was at least twice his size. On that small pad, it was hard to tell where one stopped and the other started.

The transport finished, the beam of light faded, and for a moment, everything seemed frozen in time.

Then Edwards screamed, the most skin-crawling scream of fear and pain Reed had ever heard.

The alien moved all of its eight legs at the same time, whipping them up and around, knocking into Edwards and the walls.

Reed and his two men fired.

The shots, set to stun, hit and knocked out both Edwards and the creature. They both slumped to the small transporter pad, tangled together.

Reed moved over and tapped the communications link on the wall. "Reed to Dr. Phlox. I have a medical emergency. I'm bringing in Crewman Edwards and an alien captive."

"One of the creatures from the southern continent?" Phlox sounded as if he were rubbing his hands together in delight—certainly not the reaction Reed was having. The transport area smelled strongly of dead fish, and the stench was making Reed's eyes water.

"Yes, it is," Reed said, "and I do believe it's quite dangerous."

"Believe?" Phlox asked.

"It's unconscious at the moment—or it seems to be." Reed motioned for his men to get Edwards out of there. They seemed reluctant to approach the alien. He found that indicative of the alien's repulsive looks. Reed had chosen his security team for their fortitude as well as their fighting abilities.

"Well, I'll see what I can do with it," Phlox said. "Bring it all in."

"Edwards is coming first."

"Of course," Phlox said, as if they'd already discussed that. And then the com made a slight thunk as he let it go.

Reed let his side go as well, and went to help his men. The stench was so strong here it was palpable. The air was thick with it, making it hard to breathe.

Reed's men were having trouble moving the creature's hairy legs to get at Edwards. Reed reached in, grabbed Edwards' boots, and nearly recoiled as one of the alien legs brushed against his hand.

The hair was slimy.

A shudder of disgust ran through Reed, but he said nothing. He helped his men free Edwards, then put his hands on his hips. Somehow he had to get that alien to sickbay.

And he knew that it wasn't going to be a task that he would enjoy.

Captain's log.

Vulcan Subcommander T'Pol has been critical of my allowing a shuttlepod to land and collect information on the ground in one of the southern continent's alien villages. She was firmly against it to begin with, and now that there has been a problem with Crewman Edwards and an accidental abduction of one of the aliens, she is being very cold and silent. And that's saying something for a Vulcan.

I have to admit, she might have been right in this case, as she was with the Fazi. It might have been more prudent to wait and study the aliens from orbit. I am assuming that at some point in the future of Earth's exploration of space, there will be guidelines and regulations about how to make this contact.

Clearly the Vulcans have such rules. I've spent years rebelling against them, but now, in this situation, their rules are starting to make some sense. However, until this is all settled, I will not tell T'Pol I am starting to see the value in going slower with first-contact situations.

In the meantime, Dr. Phlox has informed me that he can find nothing physically wrong with Crewman Edwards. I plan on being in sickbay when Edwards wakes up. There are a number of questions I want to ask him about those aliens and how they managed to get so close to him on the surface.

SEVENTEEN

ARCHER STOOD BESIDE CREWMAN JAMAL EDWARDS' biobed. The bright lights in sickbay made the crewman's toffee-colored skin look sallow, or perhaps it was the effect of whatever had happened to him.

Sickbay itself stank of rotted fish, a smell so strong that Archer thought of asking for a breathing mask. Phlox had adjusted the environmental controls to clear out the odor, but it wasn't working as well as it was supposed to. Archer was sure the smell wasn't going to help Edwards recover.

"I am cleansing the air, but it will take a few minutes," Phlox said in his curiously cheerful singsong voice. Even when he was being serious, he sounded a little too cheerful. Hoshi had once explained to Archer that Phlox's cheerful tone came from the fact that his voice rose at the end of a sentence instead of lowered. That, she said, was an auditory clue toward good spirits, one that wasn't true of all species.

The implied cheerfulness had taken some getting

used to, and Archer still noticed it in moments of crisis.

"Those things stink," Archer said, nodding toward the alien. It looked like a dead beetle, on its back on two biobeds as far from Edwards as possible. The carapace didn't bend, so Phlox had to put a second biobed near the first just to accommodate the creature's size.

Its legs hung awkwardly at its sides and trailed along the floor, leaving a slime path every time they moved. The slime was a brown mucus color and made Archer wince.

What was even worse was the creature's face. The face hadn't been visible until the security guards had deposited the creature onto the biobed. When it was on its carapace like this, its mouth became visible. Once Archer had seen the mouth, he located the eyes, which appeared to be the same black as the carapace.

The mouth was what disgusted him, though. It was filled with wormlike larvae attached on both the upper and lower lips where teeth should be. The mouth seemed to bother the two security guards as well, because Archer caught them taking peeks at it when they thought he wasn't looking.

He returned his attention to Edwards. There were no marks on Edwards' body, no open sores or wounds. If he had viewed the video from the surface correctly, Edwards had started screaming *before* the alien reached him.

Perhaps these aliens were like skunks, throwing off a stench that stung as well as reeked. But the smell wasn't as strong here as it was near that alien.

Unfortunately, Archer knew that from personal experience.

Even though Edwards was unconscious, he still seemed agitated. His eyes were moving back and forth under his lids. When Phlox saw that, he restrained Edwards. Phlox said patients who were so upset when they rested often awoke agitated and hurt themselves before anyone could help them. Prevention, Phlox had said, was the better part of valor.

At some point, Archer would explain to Phlox that he shouldn't mix his clichés.

But not now. Levity seemed inappropriate at the moment. Archer had no idea how a simple mission to retrieve a sample had gone so very wrong.

Phlox walked away from the environmental controls and joined Archer beside Edwards.

"Not good," Phlox said.

"What's wrong with him?" Archer asked. "Besides having been surrounded by a bunch of those guys and being stunned with a plasma pistol."

"He's still agitated," Phlox said, "and he shouldn't be, considering how deeply unconscious he is. I had him hooked up to a brain monitor that is supposed to be fairly accurate for humans and it gave me readings I'm not sure I understand."

"That's why you called me here?" Archer asked.

"I called you here because I'm going to rouse him," Phlox said. "Who knows what will happen next."

Archer didn't like the sound of that at all. "Shouldn't you keep him sedated? Let him rest?"

"No," Phlox said, injecting Edwards with a blue

liquid. "We both need information and at the moment letting him awaken is the best way to get it."

Archer just stared at Edwards. If the doctor thought this was best, then letting Edwards wake up would be the course of action.

The alien hadn't moved. It wasn't even twitching. If Phlox hadn't told him it was alive, Archer would have thought it was dead.

He only hoped Edwards didn't see it.

Edwards strained against his restraints, then moaned, twisting his head back and forth a few times. He sounded and looked as if he was in pain, as if something was chasing him.

Phlox moved to check a reading on a panel beside Edwards, shaking his head as he did so.

Edwards' eyes snapped open wide, staring at something unseen above him. And then he screamed.

It was not the scream of a solid, young man who had a life ahead of him. This was a pure, deep scream of terror that sent shivers down Archer's back.

Archer moved closer to Edwards to try to reassure him, but Dr. Phlox held up his hand, signaling Archer to stay put.

Edwards took another long breath and then screamed again, fighting hard against his restraints, his eyes open and staring at the ceiling. Something was terrifying this young man deep in his soul.

"Edwards!" Archer said, his voice firm with command. "Crewman Edwards, this is the captain."

Archer's words did nothing. Edwards kept thrashing against his restraints, staring at the ceiling, and screaming.

Finally Dr. Phlox injected Edwards again and almost instantly the strain in the young man's body eased. He stopped fighting. His eyes blinked, then closed. And from his still-open mouth came a sigh.

"Well, that worked," Archer said. "I'm now much clearer on what happened."

Phlox was still looking at the readings. "You got no answers, but I did. Give me some time to make sure of my findings."

"Report as soon as you can," Archer said. "I need to know what happened to him."

"I know. I have the same curiosity."

Archer nodded at the alien. "Should he be restrained as well?"

"I'm not sure it is a 'he,' " Phlox said. "I'm not certain these creatures have gender divisions. I've seen no indication one way or another, although I must admit, I haven't had a lot of time to study its physiology."

"Whatever it is," Archer said, determined not to be sidetracked, "should we restrain it?"

"No." Phlox sounded confident. "With two armed guards, it isn't going anywhere. And, from what I can tell, that creature won't come around for some time."

"You can't even tell if it's male or female," Archer said. "How can you figure out its level of consciousness?"

Phlox gave Archer a grin. "Some things are easier to determine than others."

Archer shook his head. "Okay. I'll trust you on this one. But I want to be here when that thing wakes up."

"I'll notify you as soon as it twitches."

"Thanks," Archer said.

With one more look at the slack-jawed Edwards, Archer turned and headed for the bridge. Everyone on this ship knew this mission was dangerous. But he didn't want to lose anyone just because he was in a hurry to have a first contact.

He didn't tolerate carelessness in his subordinates. He certainly didn't tolerate it in himself.

Captain's log.

I've taken the best and the brightest to be the Enterprise crew. People who've withstood Starfleet training and rigors that would make the average person cry. Psychological testing that bordered on inhumane and risk-aversion studies that seemed to go on forever.

Not all of my crew scored in the top ten percent of those tests, but the ones who didn't usually had a specialized skill that I couldn't do without.

Jamal Edwards, as valuable a crewman as he is, wasn't chosen for his special skills. He was chosen for his courage, his ability to take risks, his personal strength.

The fact that a man like that could be reduced to this in a matter of seconds baffles me. I have never seen such terror in a person's eyes. It was as if he was being chased through the very depths of hell.

I can barely wait for the results of Dr. Phlox's tests. I want the answers now. The damned impatience is rearing its ugly head again.

I'd been so patient waiting to get to space and now that we're here, I want to do everything at once. But I don't want to risk my crew, and that seems to be what I'm doing.

I have no idea how this has come about. The mission was a simple one. Nothing should have happened.

The alien from the southern continent that we inadvertently captured is still unconscious and I honestly have no idea what to do with it. I'm half tempted to just put it on the transporter pad and beam it back to the surface and pretend nothing happened. So far I have resisted the temptation.

I'm hoping that we'll learn something through this alien or about this alien that will help us. I'm not sure what that something will be.

Oddly enough, what bothers me the most is not what happened to Edwards, but my last conversation with the Fazi. In hindsight, the conversation feels like another warning that I should have heeded.

That conversation ended when I mentioned the other race. There's a connection between the Fazi's reaction and what happened to Edwards. I know it, deep in my bones, but I also know that this feeling is a hunch, a hunch that—at the moment—doesn't seem to be based on any concrete evidence.

I'm tempted to contact the Fazi again, but I won't. Not until I know exactly what went wrong in that last conversation. I'm not going to operate on the assumption that the Fazi were offended by my mention of the other race only to learn later that they found my head movement inappropriate.

I have T'Pol and Ensign Hoshi working as hard as they can searching through the Fazi history and language to see if they can discover anything. So far they are both very disturbed at the fact that to the Fazi, neither the southern continent nor the aliens living there exist.

T'Pol even managed to get a map from a Fazi library database and there was no southern continent on it. This is either the worst case of mass denial I could have ever imagined, or there is something far stranger happening on this planet.

EIGHTEEN

IT SEEMED LIKE THE ENTIRE SHIP SMELLED FAINTLY OF rotting fish. The odor had clung to everything since Elizabeth Cutler had returned from the planet the day before. The smell even followed her to the mess. Last night, she hadn't been able to eat dinner—no surprise, Mayweather had said, given what had happened on the planet.

He seemed calmer about it than she was, but she knew that was an act. When she'd seen him in the mess this morning, he'd had shadows under his eyes, and she could tell he'd slept as well as she had, which was hardly at all.

The entire day had been very frustrating. She had asked both Dr. Phlox and the captain if she could visit Edwards, and they'd both refused. Neither would say what was wrong with him. She had a hunch they didn't know.

What had happened in those moments on the

planet? Was it something she and Mayweather could have prevented?

Those questions had been going through her mind ever since she got back. They even interrupted her work during her duty shift. She had been studying the bits of the building she'd brought back, trying to determine how creatures built like spiders made buildings that looked like igloos.

So far she had had no luck.

After dinner, she had planned to go back to her station to look up information on spiders of all types, but her immediate commander had forbidden it.

"Elizabeth," she had said, "you look exhausted. The best thing you can do is take your mind off everything, and rest."

But she couldn't rest, and her mind was working overtime. So when Novakovich, somewhat oblivious of the events of the past two days (he'd been out of touch since he was placed on light duty), asked if they were playing the game that night, she said she would if everyone else wanted to.

Apparently they did. Anderson had shown up for dinner, but Mayweather hadn't. He had come into the mess as most of their shift's members were finishing their meals, taken a chocolate-chip cookie from the plate left beside the coffee, and hadn't even touched that.

"You have to eat," she had said to him quietly.

He'd given her a small smile. "I know," he said. "I will. Maybe after the game."

Maybe. Just like she might sleep after the game. They had gone through this routine before, after the last away mission they'd been on together, the one where Novakovich had gotten hurt. Cutler had barely slept for three days upon their return and Mayweather had hardly eaten. Both of them had consulted Dr. Phlox, who hadn't seemed too upset by it.

"You're processing," he said. "We all process differently and sometimes that means that something else will lose significance while the brain is full of new matters it must assess. What you need to do is find diversions—not that this ship has many of them. *Healthy* diversions. I would suggest a hobby of some sort, whatever interests you and has nothing to do with your work."

In some ways, the role-playing game had nothing to do with work, but in other ways, it mirrored work too closely. Cutler spread the towel on the table that Anderson had just cleared. At least she wasn't "exploring" Mars. At least she was designing it. That was different enough.

Mayweather had put his coffee and his cookie on a nearby table. Novakovich already had his padd out. His skin was looking better today, less inflamed. He seemed calmer too, and Cutler couldn't help wondering if it was because of Edwards. Now Novakovich wasn't the only one who had had trouble on an away mission and a bad transporter experience. Now he could share that experience with Edwards.

If Edwards ever got better.

Anderson came back to the table and grabbed his padd. Cutler was surprised that even with all the activity going on, and the alien in sickbay, the four of them could find time to continue the game. It seemed the ship, at least for the moment, had settled back into a routine as the crew searched for information about this planet and the two races.

Anderson rubbed his hands together. "Let's go," he said.

Cutler made sure there were enough bolts in the cup and that the paint hadn't chipped off any of them. "Do you remember where we are?"

"We're way up in this building," Novakovich said, "facing a sky bridge that is clearly a nesting place for flying Martian lizards. Right?"

"That's right," Cutler said, putting the cup of painted bolts in the middle of the folded towel. She was glad she had invented flying lizards instead of, say, giant spiders.

In spite of herself, she shuddered.

"So what are our choices?" Mayweather asked. He seemed to be watching her closely. He must have noticed the shudder. She gave him a grateful smile.

"You can either try to go across," she said, "or you can go back down. Four floors below there are two other sky bridges, but they are not as direct a route toward your goal."

"I say we give this one a try," Anderson said.

"Well," Mayweather said, "if you're so certain, go first."

Novakovich nodded.

"All right," Anderson said, "I'm moving out onto the bridge. What do I face?"

Cutler described to him how the floor of the bridge was weak, that there was debris from a

Martian flying lizard's nest directly ahead, and that he would have to try to climb through. Her description wasn't as good as usual, and she knew it. For the first time since they started playing, she wasn't able to visualize her invented Mars.

"You can still turn back safely," she said.

Anderson shook his head. "I'm going to try to climb through the nest."

Cutler handed him the cup of dice. "Six or above and you make it."

He shook the cup of bolts, making a number of people at other mess tables glance his way, shake their heads, and go back to what they were doing.

He dumped the bolts out onto the towel.

Mayweather and Novakovich both started laughing. He had rolled only one red bolt.

Anderson braced himself in the chair. "This isn't as bad as it looks, right?"

Cutler didn't answer him directly. She had learned not to do that during the game. Instead, she described what happened.

"In climbing through the nest you have stepped into a hole in the deck of the sky bridge and fallen through." She tapped the one red bolt. "You have managed to grab a beam with one hand and are hanging there."

"Can we help him?" Mayweather asked.

Cutler scooped up the bolts, put them in the cup, and dumped them out. Three red. "No. You can't."

"So what do I do?" Anderson said. "I don't want to lose Dr. Mean."

"He has to try to climb back up." Cutler put the

bolts back in the cup and handed it to Anderson. "If you roll more than your strength, you can't make it."

"Six or under then," Anderson said.

He was about to dump out the bolts when the ship's alarms went off. Cutler jumped. Mayweather's arm shot backward, and knocked over his coffee cup. The alarms were so loud Cutler couldn't hear it clatter to the floor.

Lieutenant Reed's voice came over the intercom. "The alien has escaped from sickbay. Do not try to engage. Everyone stay clear."

"Oh, my god," Cutler said.

"What can this thing do?" Novakovich asked.

"That's the problem," Mayweather said. "We really don't know."

NINETEEN

ARCHER HAD BEEN ON HIS WAY BACK TO SICKBAY WHEN Reed sounded the alarm. Even before Reed finished his announcement, Archer took off. He ran as fast as he could, ducking through the hatchways, and sliding around corners.

It took him less than a minute to reach sickbay, but he didn't go in. As he rounded the last corner, he saw both Reed and Dr. Phlox standing to one side of the corridor, clearly taking cover.

The smell of rotted fish seemed even more powerful than before. Archer almost felt as if he could see it as a clear blue haze filling the darkened corridor.

Inside sickbay, someone screamed. The cry sent chills down Archer's spine.

"What's going on?" he asked as he slid to a stop beside his chief of security.

Reed didn't look at Archer. Instead, he kept his gaze on the corridor, and the sickbay door.

"The alien woke up a bit sooner than expected," Reed said.

"I was out of the room," Dr. Phlox said, "and so was the lieutenant. We were talking about the need for more guards—"

"When my men started screaming." Reed's face was pale. "I glanced inside. The alien was moving its legs, trying to stand, like an upended turtle, and my men were clutching their heads, screaming, just like Edwards did on the surface."

Archer frowned at the sickbay door. What was going on in there?

"I came out here to prevent Dr. Phlox from going inside. He convinced me to stay beside him, and that's when I sounded the alarm." Reed ran a hand through his hair. "I must admit it didn't take convincing."

"He wanted to go in there, rifle blazing," Phlox said. "Since I'm not sure what's causing this reaction, I warned him not to."

"Sensible, Doctor," Archer said. He didn't want to lose Reed to this creature's strange powers. He was glad Phlox had stepped in.

Another scream echoed. This one was ragged, higher-pitched, and so full of terror that the hair on the back of Archer's neck stood up. That had never happened to him before. He'd always thought it was an expression instead of an involuntary response.

"All right," he said, wondering what it was about the tone of that scream that made his body react so strongly while his mind remained calm. "What are our options?"

"I've established a perimeter," Reed said. "I didn't

want to hazard more men inside sickbay. I believe we have a better chance at this creature if we wait for it to emerge. There are men on the other side of the corridor. If the alien comes out of sickbay, it can only go two ways, and we have both of those ways blocked."

The scream started again, only this time it became a wail that seemed to go on forever.

"I'm not so worried about it escaping," Archer said. "I just don't want anyone hurt, including the alien. Understood? Knock it out only."

"I've already given that order," Reed said. "All of our weapons are set on stun."

At that moment the scream cut off suddenly, leaving the corridor in total silence. Archer had never heard anything as bad as that silence. It was different from the silence he'd encountered on the planet.

That silence was an absence of sound.

This one seemed more potent than that. It seemed to hang in the air, as if it had form and substance. Archer didn't want to allow himself to think about what that silence meant to the men inside that room.

At that moment, a pair of hairy black legs eased into the corridor. Reed tensed beside Archer. Archer pulled out his own pistol.

The carapace came next, the creature's face almost completely hidden in blackness. If Archer hadn't known where the eyes were, he wouldn't have seen them, glinting darkly in the corridor's yellow light.

Archer knew that the creature's gaze didn't dare land on them. Reed must have come to the same conclusion, because he and Archer fired at the same time.

From the other side of the corridor, more shots hit the creature.

It slumped to the floor and its eyes closed.

Again the silence seemed to weigh on Archer, pushing him downward. The smell had grown so strong that it coated Archer, became part of him. He wondered if it would ever wash off.

Archer eased toward the alien, with Reed on his left, both of them keeping their weapons trained on it.

Then, inside the sickbay, a man again started to scream.

Phlox pushed past them. "Excuse me, I have a patient calling me."

He stepped over the still body of the alien as if it didn't bother him at all.

Archer glanced at Reed, who only shrugged. They crouched beside the creature. Its legs had slid outward, leaving the same slime that Archer had noticed before. He avoided the slime, stepped between the legs, and peered at the creature itself.

It seemed vulnerable, although he had no idea why he had that sense.

"I'm going to need help in here," Dr. Phlox shouted.

Reed headed into sickbay. Archer stood, reluctant to leave the creature. He motioned to the guards at the other end of the corridor.

"If it moves," he said to them, "stun it again."

They nodded. They looked as nervous as Reed had. Those screams were enough to unsettle anyone.

Archer stepped inside the sickbay and stopped. The normally clean, well-lit place looked as though a tornado had gone through it. One of the biobeds was tilted—only the fact that it was bolted into the floor had kept it from falling entirely—and a screen above was cracked. The tilted bed was covered with slime, as was the floor leading out of the sickbay.

But that wasn't what surprised Archer. He had expected some destruction. He had also expected to see bloody and wounded men.

What he actually saw was worse. One guard, Crewman Pointer, lay on the floor, away from the slime, curled in a fetal position. His hands covered his head as he rocked back and forth. His lips were moving, but no words were coming out.

The other guard, Crewman Daniels, stood, frozen in the middle of the room, his gun still in his hand. He was staring at the ceiling.

Daniels was the one who was screaming. The screams came in bursts, as if he were continually startled by something.

"You want to make sure he doesn't shoot me?" Dr. Phlox shouted at Archer over the screams.

Daniels didn't seem to hear him. Just breath after breath, he kept screaming and staring at something Archer couldn't see.

Archer and Reed pointed their plasma pistols at Daniels. Archer double-checked to make sure his was set on stun. He was amazed at the sight before him. He kept thinking about all those psychological tests, about how Reed's security team had rated the highest in Starfleet on courage and other scores, and how quickly they were reduced to this.

What were they facing?

Phlox moved around Daniels, being stealthy, although Archer doubted that was needed. Daniels seemed oblivious of everything except whatever he was seeing on the ceiling. Archer had looked up and seen nothing but the familiar white lights that usually made this room so bright and cheerful.

With one quick movement, Phlox gave Daniels a shot in the arm. Daniels didn't move. The shot didn't even interrupt his screams.

Then, suddenly, he stopped screaming. His eyes rolled into his head and he slumped to the floor. Phlox caught him just before Daniels' head hit the hard deck.

Then Phlox moved over and gave Crewman Pointer a shot, knocking him out as well.

Archer let out a breath. His ears rang. He hadn't realized how prevalent the screaming had been, like the stench that still filled this area. He wasn't sure if the smell wasn't as strong in here; it had coated his nose so badly everything stank of rotted fish.

He glanced at the alien body in the doorway, then at the two men on the floor. One alien and three of his men down, and he had no idea why.

He wasn't even sure that what he had just witnessed had been a fight. It felt more like he was being a guard in a mental ward, controlling unruly patients. And he didn't like that feeling at all.

Reed helped Phlox lift Daniels to one of the biobeds. Next to him, Edwards slept on, completely oblivious of everything that had happened around him.

Archer went to Pointer. The man's body was rigid, even though he was unconscious. His fingers twitched convulsively at his hair.

Reed came to his side, and together they carried Pointer to a nearby biobed. Phlox fluttered between both of the new patients, more upset than Archer had ever seen him.

Archer glanced at the readings above Edwards' head. They looked no different than they had before. He couldn't figure them out; he wasn't even sure what normal looked like on this equipment.

"Doctor, you said you got some answers for me when we woke up Edwards," Archer said.

"I said I got some information, not answers." Phlox was trying to ease Pointer's hands away from his head. He wasn't having much luck.

"You're going to have to convert that information into answers," Archer said. "We're out of time."

"I know." Phlox didn't look at him.

"I want all your efforts spent on figuring out what happened here," Archer said. "I want a solution, and I want it fast."

Phlox nodded.

Archer turned to Reed. "Make sure the alien stays out cold and in confinement until we know what happened here."

"Yes, sir," Reed said.

"At the first sign of trouble with that alien, I want our people to fall back, just like we did. Whatever happened to these men happened quickly and because they were within a certain proximity. You and Dr. Phlox managed to avoid the same fate, just as Ensigns Cutler and Mayweather did. I have to believe, until someone proves otherwise, that distance had something to do with it."

"Begging your pardon, sir, we don't know what caused this."

Archer gave him a cold smile. "And that's the real problem, isn't it?"

He didn't wait for a response. He stepped past the alien and headed down the corridor for the bridge. There were answers. And he had a hunch the Fazi might just have them.

TWENTY

THE SMELL FOLLOWED ARCHER TO THE BRIDGE. HE WON-
dered if it was on him or just clogging his nostrils, the
way some heavy scents did. Well, he wasn't going to
worry about it for now. His bridge crew would have to
deal with the stench if, indeed, it was trailing him.

Everyone was at their posts. Mayweather sat at the
pilot's station. Mayweather had gone off shift not
long before, but alert status had brought him back to
his position on the bridge.

The whoop of the alert alarm sounded louder
here, perhaps because it wasn't competing with
Daniels' screams.

Archer headed for his command chair. "Stand
down from alert status. Inform everyone to return to
normal schedules until notified."

Hoshi repeated the order through the intercom
system to the ship and then turned back to her
screen, clearly intent on something she was studying.
She hadn't taken any more time from the bridge than

a few short naps and meals since this all started. She had rings under her eyes and her hair was a mess, but Archer said nothing to her. He needed her to figure out what was happening, and why his mention of the race on the southern continent had made them cut off communication. One important way was through the Fazi language.

"Those of you who were off duty," Archer said to his bridge crew, "can return to your cabins. Make sure the second team gets up here. I want you all awake and sharp when you report for duty at 0600."

Several members of the bridge crew nodded. Hoshi made the announcement about regular shifts again, and behind Archer, the lift door opened as the evening crew reported back for duty.

He was still tense and angry. Nothing should have happened to his men standing guard in sickbay. It had been pure luck that whatever had attacked them had avoided Dr. Phlox. Next time, the ship might not be so lucky—and without Phlox, they would be in real trouble.

The lift door opened again, and Trip got off. He went to one of the workstations, pushing buttons and checking a screen. Supposedly he was off duty as well, but the alert had obviously put him back in work mode. At least he wasn't in engineering, worrying about the warp drive.

After a few minutes, Archer would tell Trip to relax. Until then, he could stay on the bridge and finish whatever he was working on.

Archer stood, too restless to stay in place. He walked toward T'Pol's science station. She had also spent a lot of extra time on the bridge lately, yet she looked her normal controlled self. Her nostrils flared as he came close. He suppressed a smile. He had forgotten about the Vulcan female's sensitivity to smell.

Apparently the stench that had followed him to the bridge didn't just coat his nostrils. He decided to ignore it, glad for once that protocol forbade anyone to mention the fact that he smelled like fish guts.

Like it or not, T'Pol had more experience with other races than he did. She might have encountered something like this before. With that in mind, he outlined what had happened in sickbay.

"Do you have any idea what happened in there?"

"The incident in sickbay sounds similar to the incident with Crewman Edwards on the planet," she said.

"Yeah," Archer said. "I got that much."

She didn't seem offended by his tone. Instead, she tapped a few keys and the images of Edwards and the aliens came up. "I do not believe this was an attack."

Archer stared at the screen. Edwards was holding his head and screaming, his eyes filled with terror. Fortunately the sound was off, but his anguish was plain. The aliens were approaching him, one in front and the others close behind.

"It looks like an attack to me," Archer said.

"Me, too," Trip said from behind him, and Archer jumped. He hadn't noticed Trip, and that wasn't like him.

Trip saw the reaction and grinned at him. "What, Cap? Didn't you think anyone would come close when you're wearing that lovely new cologne?"

So it did smell as bad as he feared. "No," Archer said. "Just a little too focused, I guess."

"The alien scent is pungent," T'Pol said, "although so far as I can tell it has no other dangerous properties."

"I didn't even touch it," Archer said. "I just stood near it."

"Apparently," T'Pol said, "that was enough."

"Or too much, depending on your point of view," Trip said. He pointed at the screen, his finger brushing the small image of the closest alien. "I still don't see how you can say this wasn't an attack. They approached him, he's in pain, and we have an emergency beam-out. Seems like an attack to me."

"One always makes assumptions based on one's own culture," T'Pol said, her nostrils still flaring.

Archer noted the intended insult and decided to ignore it. "Since your culture's different," he said, "what assumption are you making?"

She looked at him sideways, tilting her head up so that she could see him. She was such a formidable presence, he often forgot how small she really was.

"Vulcans do not make assumptions," she said.

Trip snorted. "Vulcans make assumptions all the time. They assume they know more than anyone else, they assume they're superior—"

Archer held up his hand for silence. "This isn't the time or place."

"Vulcans," T'Pol continued as if she hadn't been interrupted, "make informed opinions based on logic and observation."

"Logic and observation," Trip repeated as if he didn't believe it.

"What is your informed opinion?" Archer asked, struggling to keep the sarcasm from his own voice.

T'Pol leaned toward the screen. Archer got the sense that she was also leaning away from the smell.

She pointed at the lead alien. "You will note that it is not carrying anything, and it is not moving as fast as the other aliens. The others appear to be trying to catch up."

"So?" Trip asked before Archer had the chance to do the same.

"So," T'Pol said, her voice controlled and yet somehow still showing contempt in the single word, "I would consider the possibility that they were simply coming to greet a stranger."

Archer stared at the screen. Greeting a stranger calmly was what a Vulcan would do. But he couldn't ignore Edwards.

"I'd agree with you," Archer said, "if Edwards weren't screaming."

T'Pol crossed her arms and tilted her head up toward him. Her nostrils still flared and her greenish skin tone seemed more pronounced than usual.

"Many things can disturb a person," she said. "While they are unpleasant, they are not always an attack."

"Like what?" Trip asked.

"Smells," T'Pol said with a delicacy that Archer had to admire. "They assault the senses, sometimes drive sensitive people to illness, but the smell is not always intentional."

"On Earth, we have animals that spray their scents, sometimes to mark territory, sometimes to keep predators away," Archer said.

"Yet you are covered with an odor that was not sprayed upon you as a deliberate territorial marking or as a defense," T'Pol said.

"And it offends you," Archer said with a hint of a smile.

"I am sure I am not alone," she said calmly.

"She's got you there, Captain," Trip said.

"Some species react so strongly to smells that they pass out when the smell is particularly strong," T'Pol said. "Others suffer through watery eyes and swelled mucous membranes. Still others get physically ill almost immediately. All of these reactions might look to an outsider like a reaction to an attack—and technically, they are. They are an attack on the senses, but the attack is not a deliberate one."

Archer frowned and looked at the screen again. "It has bothered me that they never touched him."

"Yeah," Trip said, "and there are no signs of weapons—at least not any we recognize."

T'Pol inclined her head forward as an acknowledgment of what they were saying. "We see what we expect to see. If we assume this is an attack, we look for invisible weapons, other methods of hurt. If we assume this is a welcoming party, then we have another dilemma."

"I can tell you right now, no human reacts to a strong smell that way," Archer said.

"Clearly," T'Pol said dryly. "But I do not think smell is the problem here, although I do believe that Crewman Edwards suffered an assault on his senses."

"What kind of assault?" Archer asked.

"An unintentional one, just as your cologne, as Engineer Tucker calls it, is assaulting mine."

"They're doing something to him that's as natural to them as breathing?" Archer asked, trying to follow this.

"In a word," T'Pol said.

"What would that something be?" Trip asked.

"Telepathy," T'Pol said.

"These spider-folks are telepathic?" Trip asked.

"What informs this opinion of yours?" Archer asked.

"Logic," T'Pol said.

"That's as good an answer as if I said my idea of an attack was based on a hunch," Trip said.

But Archer wasn't as convinced. "I want to hear this," he said to Trip. Then he nodded at T'Pol. "Explain this logic to me."

"Telepathy would function just as well on land as under water," she said. "It would be a logical development for creatures who need to exist in both environments."

Hoshi stood and moved to join the discussion. She looked intrigued for the first time in days. "I understand there are a few races that employ limited telepathic communications."

T'Pol nodded. "I have heard of such telepathic races, but never had the pleasure of encountering one."

"Pleasure?" Trip asked. "I don't think Edwards considers what he is going through a pleasure."

Archer agreed. Edwards had screamed like he was in hell.

T'Pol looked at the chief engineer. "I believe the

only luck we've had here is that a human crewman was not killed by a telepathic encounter."

Trip started to say something, but Archer stopped him with a wave of the hand again.

"What makes you say that?" Archer asked T'Pol.

"I do not believe the human mind can withstand a telepathic encounter. Humans lack the ability to control their most simple thoughts."

"Even if I were to accept that statement as true, which I do not," Archer said, "what does controlling thoughts have to do with telepathy?"

"A weaker mind cannot block a telepathic encounter if the mind cannot block its own random thoughts," T'Pol said. "The level of control needed to withstand an invasive thought is considerable, especially if that invasive thought comes from the outside."

Archer was about to argue when Hoshi took a step closer.

"That might explain the rigid thought and cultural structure of the Fazi," Hoshi said, more to herself than anyone else.

T'Pol nodded. "It would be a logical development of a culture in close planetary contact with a telepathic race."

"Huh?" Trip said.

"I think this does need some explanation," Archer said.

Hoshi turned to him, her face animated. "The theories on telepathy hold that without control, it will drive someone mad. So in order to use telepathy as a communication device, the minds involved must be completely restrained, structured and guarded."

"Precisely," T'Pol said. "Vulcans have developed limited telepathic ability in certain circumstances, partially due to our control of our emotions."

Archer gave her a sideways glance. He'd heard rumors that Vulcans had telepathic abilities, but the abilities were considered so personal, so private, that humans had been cautioned not to talk with Vulcans about it.

He was amazed that T'Pol had brought this up on her own. She was probably doing so because he had goaded her on her own assumptions.

"Let me see if I'm clear on this," Archer said. "The alien we stunned was only trying to talk to Edwards and the other two crewmen?"

"It would be logical, considering the circumstances and what we observed on the surface," T'Pol said.

"And by trying to talk to our men," Trip said, "the alien did something to their brains?"

"If what we postulate about the telepathic communication is true," T'Pol said, "then the logical conclusion is that the human mind is not structured enough to handle telepathic thought."

"And your brain is structured enough?" Trip asked, clearly getting angry.

"Yes," T'Pol said.

That was enough. Archer didn't want to hear the bickering at the moment. "We're still operating on assumption here. There's no way to prove that was a benign telepathic communication. For all we know, it could have been a telepathic attack—or something else equally invisible, such as a sound that caused damage while being outside the register of the human ear or, as T'Pol has already reminded us, a smell."

T'Pol raised a single eyebrow.

"I still consider your theory a hunch, T'Pol," Archer said.

She stiffened and he realized he had offended her. He didn't care.

"I'm not willing to risk your mind. I don't want you to try to talk to this alien, no matter how structured your thoughts are. There has to be another way and I want you people to find it. Understand?"

Hoshi and Trip nodded. T'Pol inclined her head again.

"Now would be a good time," Archer said, glaring at them.

Hoshi returned to her station. Trip grinned and headed to the lift. Archer hadn't moved. T'Pol was watching him, still leaning away slightly.

"T'Pol," Archer said, "I want you to inform Dr. Phlox of your theory. See if he believes it will help with the affected crewmen."

"I will do so at once." She walked around him and headed for the lift. He wasn't sure if it was his imagination or not, but she seemed to be moving faster than usual.

He needed to leave as well, get cleaned up, and then come back to the bridge. He felt as if they were close to solving this, even though he didn't completely buy T'Pol's telepathy explanation. The problem with logic was that it always sounded so appealing and wasn't always right.

Still, it seemed as plausible if not more plausible than the attack theory.

Archer turned and stared at the big screen. The Fazi planet slid by. From orbit it seemed like such a normal, peaceful world. But it was far from that. And for the first time, Archer understood how easy the Vulcans had it when they came to Earth.

TWENTY-ONE

IT FELT ODD TO RETURN TO THE GAME. CUTLER'S HEART was still pounding double-time, and she'd had nothing to do during the alert. In fact, she had just gone back to her quarters when Mayweather had contacted her.

"Now I'm hungry," he said. "Can we play while I have dinner?"

"If the others agree," she had said. Apparently they had, because she had set up the table for the second time that night. Anderson, Novakovich, and Mayweather had their padds ready.

Mayweather was eating some sort of sandwich he'd concocted out of the leftovers that the crew was allowed to dig in. It was huge and dripping with various multicolored juices. She recognized pickles, a white cheese, and some kind of tomato, but nothing else looked familiar. She hoped the thick brown slab in the middle was meat, but she couldn't tell from this distance.

To his credit, Mayweather turned and took bites

off the sandwich away from the playing table. Anderson, who had taken a cookie while Mayweather was making his sandwich, was chomping away merrily, getting crumbs all over the towel.

"Okay," Anderson said around the cookie, spraying even more crumbs as he spoke, "we left me hanging, literally, when the alert went off."

In spite of herself, Cutler smiled. "We left Dr. Mean hanging from his fingers under a Martian sky bridge."

Slowly, other members of the crew were trickling in. They were going back to their meals and conversations, with little discussion about the alien. Cutler was surprised at how this crew seemed to take such things in stride already.

"Can these guys help me?" Anderson asked.

"We went through that already," Cutler said.

Anderson's eyes twinkled. "Just seeing if you remembered that."

"The game master knows all, sees all," Cutler said.

"I sure hope not," Novakovich said, and winked. He was obviously beginning to feel better.

"Can I climb back up?" Anderson asked.

"That's a strength maneuver," Mayweather said.

"Better strength than brains," Anderson said. "Mean isn't very strong, but he is extremely dumb."

Cutler had designed this trap to be difficult. She had a minus two around it in her notes. "You have to roll to see how hard this is to escape from. If it takes more than four red to escape, you will fall."

"Come on, babies," Anderson said to the bolts. "Let's hide that red."

"You know, talking to bolts just seems weird," Novakovich said to Mayweather.

"People talk to dice," Mayweather said.

"Yeah, but that's tradition. Bolts—"

Anderson rolled. Red after red bolt appeared on the white towel.

"Seven," Cutler said. "You have fallen to your death."

Anderson stood. "My death! You said nothing about my death. You just said I was going to fall!"

"Would you have done something differently if you knew you were going to fall to your death?" Cutler asked.

"I don't know," Anderson said. "I just think you have it out for me. I've died twice."

"Now, how often do you hear that sentence?" Mayweather whispered to Novakovich.

"You guys go ahead and laugh," Anderson said. "Wait until you die. It's not fun."

"Depends on your point of view," Novakovich said and grinned.

Anderson shook his head. "Am I out of the game now?"

"Of course not," Cutler said. "You can roll a new character."

"Will he be hanging off the sky bridge too?" Anderson asked, hands on his hips.

"No, actually," Cutler said. "He'll have to go back to the beginning."

"I'll be running behind these guys trying to catch up?"

"Maybe we'll wait for you," Mayweather said.

Cutler suppressed a smile. If they even tried that, she'd sic the Martian flying lizards on them.

"Would you?" Anderson asked, sounding like a little kid.

"If you give us half the profits," Novakovich said.

"Who says there are profits in this game?" Anderson asked.

"Well, what do we get when we find the treasure?" Novakovich asked.

"A complete Universal Translator," Mayweather said. "I'm sure we can sell it to someone."

"That's a long way away," Cutler said. "You're only looking for a piece of it now."

"You could quit," Novakovich said, "but that's no fun."

Anderson frowned. "All right," he said, sitting down. "I'll roll a new character."

"Technically," Cutler said, "your turn's over."

"Oh, let him roll," Mayweather said as he turned away from the table. He picked up his sandwich and something lime green slipped from it to the floor.

As he bent down to retrieve it, Cutler handed Anderson the cup of bolts. Anderson rolled his new character, whom he called Horseman. Horseman had an eight strength, an intelligence of three, charisma of one, dexterity of six, and luck of three.

"They're getting dumber and stronger," Novakovich said.

"I could have used the strength the last time," Anderson mumbled.

"You could have used the smarts the last time,"

Mayweather said. "I'm sure there was some other way off that bridge."

There was, but Cutler wasn't going to tell them what it was. The other two might face the same problem later.

"I need another cookie," Anderson said, and got up. "Anybody want anything?"

The other two shook their heads.

"I guess one of you gets to take a turn," Cutler said. "What do you want to do?"

Mayweather wiped pale pink goo off his mouth, finished chewing, and said, "I don't want to get on that bridge. Let's go back down a number of floors to the other sky bridges."

"Sounds good to me," Novakovich said.

She rolled the bolts and came up with five. "You made it safely down the stairs and to the sky bridges. You have two choices. Go either to the left or right. The right leads to a building that seems shorter and only has one other sky bridge headed out of it toward the center of the city. To the left there is another tall building, with a number of choices, but none leading to the center of the city."

"Left," they said in unison. And after a quick roll they made it safely across.

Anderson came back with five cookies. He gave one to everyone and kept two for himself.

"It's your turn," Cutler said to him as she set her cookie on the table behind her. She didn't eat chocolate-chip, but she wasn't going to tell him that. It was a nice gesture. "You're back at the beginning. Does your character want to cross that canal?"

Anderson thought about it for a moment. "You mean I could take a different route?"

"Sure," Cutler said.

"Would I be able to rejoin the team?"

She shrugged.

"I'm crossing the canal," he said.

"Okay," she said. "Do you want to take the boat or try to cross the bridge?"

"Cross the bridge," he said.

"All right," she said. "Now remember there's a hole a third of the way in—"

"Like I'm about to forget," Anderson said. "A man doesn't forget where he faced death the first time."

He said that jokingly, but Cutler shivered. She thought about that moment on the planet when Edwards started screaming, the way she felt leaning out of the shuttlepod, the wind in her face, and Edwards below, still screaming, the alien approaching him.

Her gaze met Mayweather's. He gave her a shaky smile. Apparently he'd been thinking the same thing.

Anderson and Novakovich were staring at her. She realized it was her turn to do something.

Cutler glanced at her notes. "The plank is still there, covering the hole."

"Good," Anderson said. "Then I'll cross it."

Cutler handed him the cup of bolts. "Same roll as before. Anything more than two red bolts and Horseman makes it."

Anderson nodded and shook the cup, causing a few nearby diners to glance their way. Then he tipped the cup upside down on the towel.

One red bolt.

Mayweather and Novakovich burst into laughter.

"Oh, not again," Anderson said.

"Horseman," Cutler said carefully so that she wouldn't laugh too, "has fallen off the plank—"

"And into the water below. Gee whiz. How did I know that?" Anderson asked.

"Sploush!" Mayweather said, and laughed harder.

"And now I suppose there are Martian sea creatures after me again," Anderson said.

"We need to see if he survived the fall," Cutler said.

"Doom survived the fall," Anderson said. "If he survived the fall, then Horseman could survive it. He's the strongest character I have had *so far.*"

He said those last two words with painful emphasis.

"I suppose you're right," Cutler said, without checking. "He survived."

"And I'm swimming for shore," Anderson said. "Let's cut to the chase here. I want to know if my pal Horseman survives."

Cutler scooped up the bolts and placed them in the cup. "Seven or better and you get to try this bridge again."

"I'm beginning to hate bridges," Anderson mumbled as he shook the cup. The bolts rattled inside. After an inordinately long time, he upended the cup.

Three red bolts.

"A mutated Martian canal trout over fifty feet long—"

"Has bitten Horseman in half," Anderson said. "I know, I know. Horseman is dead."

"And there isn't even anyone around to mourn him," Novakovich said.

"Rub it in," Anderson said. "Wait until Rust dies. See if we mourn him."

"You gonna keep playing?" Novakovich asked.

"Of course I'm going to keep playing," Anderson said. "You don't think a measly little game can defeat me, do you? No matter how many times it kills me."

"Well, I'm not going to keep going." Mayweather actually yawned. "Laughter must be good for the soul. I'm tired for the first time in days."

"Me, too," Cutler said.

"Hey! You can't leave me here, twice dead."

" 'Fraid we're going to have to," Cutler said. "I'm taking my bolts and going to bed."

"I'm not even going to touch that line," Novakovich said as he stood up.

"Can we play tomorrow, then?" Anderson asked. "After our shifts?"

"For someone who nearly quit, you seem awfully anxious to keep playing," Mayweather said.

"I'm determined now," Anderson said. "You guys have never seen me determined."

"Oh, man. I'm scared," Novakovich said, and winked again.

"I'll have a great new character by then," Anderson said.

"I'd teach him how to swim faster," Mayweather said.

With that, they left the now empty mess, all but Anderson laughing.

TWENTY-TWO

ARCHER HAD HOPES THAT A SOLUTION MIGHT BE ON the way when Dr. Phlox called him and asked him to come to sickbay. Archer left immediately.

The smell still hovered in the corridor near sickbay, although it wasn't as strong as it was. Archer was amazed he could notice the difference; it meant that the long shower he had taken, using the industrial-strength soap he'd found in the mess, actually worked.

The floor was no longer covered with the creature's slime, and there was no evidence of the events that had taken place that afternoon. However, to Archer, they felt as recent as a few moments ago.

He walked into sickbay. Beeping and the soft sounds of equipment filled the room. Dr. Phlox stood between two biobeds, staring at the readings above them, his reddish hair tangled as if he'd been scratching the back of his head in frustration.

The three crewmen were all restrained to beds, and all seemed to be sleeping. The alien had been moved to the brig, where Reed was keeping it under guard. Phlox was supposed to report there often to make sure the alien remained unconscious.

"Any change?" Archer asked.

"None that I can tell," Dr. Phlox said.

T'Pol and Hoshi walked into the sickbay together. T'Pol's nostrils flared again, and Hoshi put a hand to her nose, before letting it fall. Apparently the smell hadn't gone down as much as Archer thought it had.

"But," Phlox continued, "I'm keeping them drugged to give their minds and bodies time to rest. For the moment I feel it is the best thing I can do for them."

"A logical treatment," T'Pol said.

But logic wasn't what Phlox was searching for. He wanted answers, as Archer did. Archer recognized the frustration in the doctor's eyes. Archer felt it himself.

"This is what I wanted to show you." Phlox brought up an image of a scanning readout on the screen over the diagnostic bed. Archer, T'Pol, and Hoshi gathered around it. "This was a continuous scan I was running on Edwards when the alien woke up."

Phlox traced a line that suddenly jumped off the chart, cutting through all the other readings that had stayed on the same basic lines. Whatever it was, it didn't look good.

"What does that mean?" Archer asked.

"I believe it's a spike in psionic energy," Dr. Phlox said. "I monitor everything I can think of with most patients I believe have brain damage."

"Psionic energy?" T'Pol asked. "I didn't realize humans had the capability to monitor such things."

Phlox gave her an amused look. "They may not,

Subcommander. But as you should note, I'm not human."

"You're working on their equipment."

"Which I sometimes modify for my own use."

T'Pol clasped her hands behind her back and stepped closer to the console, studying the lines on the screen. Hoshi was frowning.

Archer continued to watch them. He had a lot of questions, but he suspected he'd get his answers if he was just patient.

"Doctor," T'Pol said, "are you able to isolate the wave pattern of the energy from your monitors?"

"I should be able to." Phlox's fingers moved over the board in front of the monitor. Archer watched and said nothing, letting him work with T'Pol standing beside him. Behind him one of the men groaned in his sleep. Hoshi turned around, but no one else did.

"There," Phlox said. "I think that's it."

T'Pol stared at the screen for a long time. Finally she said, "Very good, Doctor."

Phlox grinned at Hoshi, who didn't smile back. T'Pol looked at all three patients, a slight frown creasing her forehead. Then she nodded once and turned to Archer.

"Captain," she said, "these readings confirm my theory that the aliens are telepathic."

From her interest alone, Archer had suspected as much. Still, he needed to know the reason for her conclusion. "What makes you think that?"

"There are as many types of telepathy as there are cultures who have traces of it," T'Pol said. "Vulcan scientists believe that even humans—who do not use most of their brains—have rudimentary telepathic abilities. Untouched, of course."

"Of course," Archer said, unable to resist the sarcasm.

She ignored his comment. "We know that some forms of telepathy use different types of psionic energy. For such energy to even register on Dr. Phlox's instrument, it must be a very strong and very concentrated beam."

"Oh." Hoshi breathed the word. "Of course."

Her "of course" was not sarcastic, as Archer's had been. Hers showed a realization.

"Of course?" Archer asked.

Hoshi nodded. "These aliens communicate underwater. Of course they'd have to use a strong and concentrated energy beam."

"Of course," Archer muttered.

Then he looked at his men, unconscious and restrained. Edwards had grabbed his head, Daniels had continued to scream, and Pointer had rolled into a fetal ball. Archer tried to imagine a concentrated beam of psionic energy entering his mind and found he couldn't do it.

Or maybe he didn't want to, given what had happened to the three crewmen.

"What kind of effect would this beam, directed at a human mind, have?" he asked Phlox.

"I am not certain," Phlox said. "But I am certain the human brain would not be able to handle it."

"At this strength, Doctor," T'Pol said, "a Vulcan brain would also have difficulty."

Archer was surprised. It wasn't often that a Vulcan

admitted a weakness. He said nothing. No point in discouraging such comments from T'Pol.

Hoshi was studying the wave pattern of psionic energy on Dr. Phlox's screen.

"Would it be possible to duplicate this wave pattern?" she asked.

"In theory, yes," T'Pol said.

"Why would we want to?" Archer asked.

"To communicate with them," Hoshi said.

"Okay, I'm lost," Archer said. Which rather annoyed him, considering that they were talking about communication and using the same language. Even when people spoke the same language, they weren't always clear. "I thought these creatures are telepathic."

"They are," Hoshi said.

"But if they are telepathic," Archer said, "do they use or need language?"

"Of course," Hoshi said. "Just not in the way we are used to it."

"This is why thoughts need to be controlled," T'Pol said. "To use telepathy as a communications device means eliminating other random thoughts and feelings. A being must be able to keep her innermost thoughts private while using telepathy to communicate. It's a difficult proposition, and it is the reason that many telepathically gifted races often turn to spoken language."

That made sense, Archer supposed. Although he really preferred to have his brain remain untouched by any other thoughts but his own. Maybe that was because he'd never experienced telepathy.

Of course, if the experience of telepathy caused

the reaction his crewmen had had, it was certainly something he never, ever wanted.

Hoshi turned to T'Pol. "Would it be possible to develop a device using these wavelengths and have that device amplify your thoughts to them carried on a psionic energy band, and then reduce the power of the energy in their thoughts to you to a level you could comfortably deal with?"

"An adapter?" Archer said. "Using the same principle they used for electric currents."

"Exactly," Hoshi said.

Archer, Hoshi, and Dr. Phlox stood watching T'Pol as she thought.

"It might be possible, yes," T'Pol said after a long moment.

"Do it," Archer said. "But I want this thing to work from a distance. I don't want to take any more chances with my crew. If there's even the slightest possibility that anyone will get hurt, T'Pol, I don't want to do this."

"I am willing to take the risk," T'Pol said.

"I am not," Archer said.

She studied him for a moment, then inclined her head once, like a queen granting a subject's request.

"Doctor," Archer said, "how much damage do you think these thought beams had on the minds of my crewmen?"

Phlox shook his head. "I have taken scans," he said. "It seems that Edwards has suffered more than the others. But whether there is damage and whether or not it is permanent, I cannot tell you."

Archer sighed and looked at them once more.

They hadn't moved. They looked peaceful, even though he suspected they were not.

Then he nodded, and headed out of sickbay. He needed to check in with Reed and make sure that the alien stayed out cold until T'Pol and Hoshi figured out a way to talk to it.

He didn't want to see another member of his crew strapped unconscious to a biobed.

TWENTY-THREE

Captain's log.

It has been over twenty hours since T'Pol and Hoshi suggested the idea of creating an adapter to communicate with the alien from the southern continent. They both assure me they are making progress, and since I understand nothing about what they are attempting, I have to believe them. How they can come up with a device that will allow T'Pol to communicate telepathically with the aliens is beyond my science skills. I have asked both of them to carefully record every detail of their work for future scientists of both cultures to study.

Dr. Phlox has reported that the three crewmen are resting easily now. Edwards, the first one the aliens tried to talk to telepathically, seems to be slowly recovering, but Dr. Phlox says it is too early to tell. Dr. Phlox be-

lieved that Edwards suffered more damage than the others because he was in closer proximity and the psionic attack, if that's the phrase we want to use, lasted longer. Also, he was surrounded by four aliens, when Daniels and Pointer only faced one.

Dr. Phlox is not allowing any of them to regain full consciousness yet. He believes their brains will heal best without inflicting the real world on them at the same time. The less they have to process the better, or so he says. He also says that sleep, whether natural or artificial, is restorative for humans no matter how healthy they are. He used that moment to lecture me on making certain the rest of my crew got enough rest.

I know that Hoshi is not getting enough. I suppose I could order her to her quarters, but I confess that I need her working right now. She and T'Pol are bearing the burden of these last few days. The rest of us seem to be reacting more than acting.

That's an unusual position for me. I like to take the initiative, but there isn't much initiative for a captain to take in this situation. I have decided not to contact the Fazi yet, and they haven't tried to contact us.

I hope they wait a little while longer, to give us a better understanding of both the Fazi culture and the alien culture that shares their world.

Waiting. I hadn't realized there was so much of it in this job. When Starfleet debriefs me after this mission is over—whenever that will be—I'm going to have to ask them to find ways to help the crew deal with downtime. Yes, they need sleep as Dr. Phlox said, but we can only sleep so much.

Because the Enterprise is so streamlined, we did not bring a lot of entertainment with us. Everyone brought favorite books, excellent recordings, and a few other items that could be digitally stored, and I know there's a lot of swapping of items going on among the crew. But I get the sense that's not enough distraction.

We don't really have a place for organized recreation. The mess hall is too small to accommodate most of the crew at one time, and a person's quarters are barely big enough for two. Hell, I feel cramped with Porthos, and he doesn't take as much space as another person—most of the time.

I hear that a few of the crew are playing a game in the mess hall. I wish others would do the same. It might take their minds off their duties long enough to help them remain creative and refreshed.

CUTLER MADE NOTATIONS IN HER PADD AS ANDERson rolled his newest character. She listened with half an ear as the bolts hit the towel. Mayweather rocked on the back two legs of his chair, and Novakovich finished the last of the cabbage soup he'd eaten for dinner.

His face was clearing up, and he looked more comfortable than he had when they started playing the game, nearly a week before. His attitude was improved as well. He smiled more. Maybe that was a function of the clearer skin. It might have been painful to smile through all the sand pimples.

The mess was crowded on this night. A lot of people had gotten off their duty shifts late. Cutler had. She had spent the day studying the files that Phlox had sent over on the alien. She had asked for permission to visit the brig to see the creature and had been denied. So she had to content herself with 3-D images and the results of someone else's scans.

Those provided a lot of information, but there was a lot she would have done differently as well. She longed for a time when she could see the alien up close and personal.

"You got a name for this one?" Mayweather asked Anderson.

"Abe," Anderson said. Even after an entire night's sleep and a full work shift, Cutler could tell that Anderson was still upset about losing his third character in the Martian canal.

"Why Abe?" Novakovich asked.

"Figured I'm going to die so many times in this silly game, I should name my characters alphabetically. So Abe it is. The next one is named Benny."

"The point is to keep the characters alive," Mayweather said.

"Oh, really?" Anderson asked. "I hadn't noticed."

Cutler laughed along with the rest of them, but it was clear Anderson wasn't really happy about the death of all his characters.

Mayweather, still leaning back in his chair, studied Anderson. From that angle, Anderson couldn't see the contemplative look on Mayweather's face. Contemplative and full of sympathy. After a moment, Mayweather's gaze met Cutler's.

"You know," he said, "why don't we just let Anderson's new character join us?" Mayweather suggested as they got ready to start.

"I have no problem with that," Novakovich said.

Novakovich and Mayweather stared at Cutler, waiting for an answer. She didn't know what to say to them. In the games she had played as a kid, you always had to start over when your character was killed. But now she was in charge and making up the rules and she could do what she wanted.

"No," Anderson said, "Abe can catch up with you."

Cutler nodded. "That is the traditional way to play," she said.

"Can he at least swim?" Mayweather asked, laughing.

"I don't know if it matters," Anderson said. "The other guys could swim and they still died."

"We don't know if Dr. Mean could swim," Novakovich said. "After all, he made it farther than the first two."

"Well, I don't really like Abe's prospects," Anderson said as he gathered up the bolts and put them into the cup.

Neither did Cutler. Of all of Anderson's characters, Abe had rolled the lowest scores. He had an intelligence of four, a strength of three, charisma of six, dexterity of eight, and a luck of two. In other words, he made friends easily, was good with his hands, and had nothing else to recommend him.

Sounded like a few guys Cutler had dated in school. She smiled at her own private joke.

"Okay," Cutler said, "where do you guys want to start?"

"The beginning is always good," Mayweather said.

"And in this case, the beginning is Anderson," Novakovich said.

"Abe," Anderson corrected. "Anderson has been to the beginning three times already."

He grabbed the cup with both hands. "You're going to let me get to the bridge with no problem, aren't you?" he said to Cutler.

She nodded. "The bridge over the canal is just like it was before. The plank is even still there."

"Thank heavens for small miracles," Anderson said. "I doubt Abe is smart enough to figure out that trick on his own."

So did Cutler, but she didn't say that. "He needs more than two red bolts to get across."

"More than," Anderson said as he shook the cup. "What happens if he only gets two?"

"He totters on that plank, trying to catch his balance, until you roll again."

"Gee, you're mean," Anderson said.

"But she's not Dr. Mean," Novakovich said.

"He's dead," Mayweather said, and chuckled.

"Not funny," Anderson said as he tossed the bolts on the table.

The group stared at them. For a moment, Cutler thought he'd rolled no red bolts at all. Then she saw the red ones at the far end.

"Three!" Anderson shouted. "I rolled three!"

People at nearby tables looked up as if Anderson had lost his mind. He was jumping up and down and screaming, "Three!"

"All that means is that you made it across," Mayweather said, looking slightly embarrassed at the display.

"Do you know how hard that is?" Anderson asked.

Mayweather shrugged. "Unk thought it was a piece of cake."

Anderson grimaced at him and sat down. Novakovich smiled and set his soup bowl on the table behind them.

"Okay," Cutler said to Anderson, "Abe is entering the city. The building where Unk and Rust are waiting is two blocks ahead, but the street is blocked by debris. You can go up into buildings on either side of the street, or take the subway."

"Which side of the street are they on?" Anderson asked.

"The right," Cutler said.

"Is there sky bridges between the buildings on that side?"

"There are," Cutler said.

"Then I'll skip them," Anderson said. "I really hate bridges."

"You're going through the debris?" Mayweather asked, sounding alarmed.

"I'll have better luck there."

"You might flush out green Martians with pointy teeth," Novakovich said.

"So what?" Anderson said. "I have a new character waiting in the wings."

He sounded flip, but didn't look that way as Cutler led him through the debris, roll by roll. The other two players waited patiently for him to pick his way across the two blocks, disturbing Martian rats and Martian red slugs, but not doing any serious damage.

Each roll of Anderson's was close. A couple of times, Cutler thought he'd failed, and then Mayweather would point out a bolt that Cutler could have sworn was unpainted a moment before. She had a hunch Mayweather was helping Anderson, and in this case she didn't mind.

In the future, she'd keep her eye on Mayweather.

"All right," she said after a torturous twenty minutes, "you've joined the others."

They let out a large cheer. The remaining diners in the mess hall stared, but didn't come over. They'd learned early in the game that RPGs were not a spectator sport.

Cutler made a notation in her padd that Anderson's trek through the debris-covered street had alerted the Martians to the players' position. She wasn't sure how she would use that, but she knew she would eventually.

"All right," she said, "let's see what Unk and Rust are going to—"

At that moment the intercom crackled. "Ensign Cutler, report to Subcommander T'Pol on the bridge at once."

For a moment, the word "bridge" blended in her mind with the bridges in the ruined city. She frowned, wondering what that meant, then grinned at herself. She had gotten very deep into the game this evening.

And now she was being summoned to work. Work. If they were calling her for an extra duty shift, that only meant one thing: she was going to be able to see the alien.

Cutler jumped to her feet and moved over to the wall of the mess and tapped the intercom button. "Ensign Cutler here. On my way."

She didn't feel she even had time to take the game pieces back to her room. She picked up the padd containing her notes. "Travis, would you take care of the towel and stuff until tomorrow?"

"Glad to," Mayweather said.

"Thanks," she said, and headed for the exit. As she did, she heard Novakovich say, "You know, Anderson, you have to stop dying, or we'll never get a chance to play."

Cutler smiled. Eventually they'd figure out the little twists and turns of the game. She could only give them so many clues—and the largest one was in the structure of the game itself. They still hadn't figured it out, and that was to her credit. That was one secret she hadn't let out, even in her inexperienced early days.

Then she got on the lift and her thoughts turned

to work. She had been hoping that her studies of the alien locked in the brig would bring her more into the main action, and it seemed that now they had.

It was time to gather information on her own.

It was time to face the alien.

TWENTY-FOUR

THE LIFT OPENED AND ARCHER SWIVELED IN HIS CHAIR. Ensign Cutler got off, a padd tucked under her arm, and purpose in her walk. It was amazing how fast his staff reported for duty when something unusual was happening. Cutler looked thrilled to be up here.

He hoped she could help them. She hadn't been able to study the creature in person. She'd only been able to use the information that Phlox had gathered. But Cutler and the other two exobiologists on the crew had been focusing on the aliens of the southern continent and their strange buildings ever since Cutler had gone on the away mission with Edwards. Archer hoped the exobiologists would have something he could use.

Cutler walked to the science station. T'Pol didn't acknowledge her—at least not right away. Neither did Hoshi, who was sitting at her communications station, one hand cupping an earpiece as she worked on the problem she and T'Pol were facing.

Cutler waited beside the science station. T'Pol finally looked up.

"Ensign," she said. "The captain and I have a request."

Archer got out of the chair and walked to the science station. He was trying to keep his pacing to a minimum, but it wasn't working. He was so restless that sitting still was a chore.

"Anything, Subcommander," Cutler said.

Archer grinned. "You should never make that offer to a Vulcan."

Cutler's eyes widened when he spoke. "S-Sorry, sir. Captain. Sir."

It always surprised him that he made the crew nervous.

"It is certainly not inappropriate to offer one's services at one's job to a Vulcan, Captain," T'Pol said with such stiffness that Archer knew he had offended her.

"It was a joke, T'Pol," Archer said.

"It was a poor one," T'Pol said. "I believe jokes should have an element of humor."

"Really?" Archer allowed himself to be distracted for a moment. "Tell me a Vulcan joke."

"Vulcans do not waste their time with such trivial things," T'Pol said.

"You mean Vulcans have no sense of humor so they see no point in joking," he said.

"That would be one interpretation," T'Pol said.

"Is there another?"

"Vulcans can be amused, Captain," she said.

Cutler watched this exchange with interest. She

seemed shocked at T'Pol's free commentary on Archer's statements.

"I thought amusement was an emotion," he said.

"Amusement can be an intellectual response to certain stimuli," T'Pol said. "In that, it is akin to curiosity, which is also a Vulcan trait."

"If you say so," Archer said. "Although I do recall a Vulcan subcommander telling me she'd spent weeks in San Francisco without visiting any of the local attractions."

T'Pol straightened. "I was there to work."

"All work and no play—"

"Puts off needed tasks," T'Pol said, facing Cutler. "Ensign, we have discussed some of your studies of the culture of the southern continent. How up to date are you on the latest developments in our contact with the alien aboard this ship?"

Cutler shrugged. "I, um, know that it's telepathic. I know that it uses psionic energy to communicate, and I know that the communication is harmful to humans. Other than that, I'm not sure what you mean, Subcommander."

"Do you find these traits unusual?" T'Pol asked.

"In spiderlike creatures or in general?"

"Either will do," T'Pol said.

"In some ways, I think it's inaccurate to call this a spiderlike creature. This creature has no arachnid traits beyond the hairy legs." Cutler's voice sounded more certain now.

Archer leaned against the station, watching. He was always amazed at the diversity of intellects within his crew.

"This creature has more in common with crustaceans," Cutler said. "It has a hard shell, like most crustaceans, and it is primarily aquatic, although it can survive in the air as well, like some kinds of crabs. But even that analogy isn't the best, since most Earth-based crustaceans need to return to the water after a certain period of time. From what I can tell, this creature does not. It can survive on land long enough to build structures, and it has certainly had no problems here—unless no one's told me about them."

"It's been unconscious most of the time," Archer said.

"I'm referring to breathing problems, sir," she said. "Or problems with the shell—flaking, drying out, that sort of thing. This is an amphibious creature, but not an amphibian."

Archer's head was beginning to spin. "What's the difference?"

"It can survive on land or in water," Cutler said, "but to be classified as an amphibian, it must have vertebrae. This creature most definitely does not."

"Okay." Biology was never really his strong suit. He got through it, but not because it held any special interest for him. Astronomy, engineering, spaceships—that was where his interest was.

"Just to be cautious," she said, "I had my team investigate arachnids, crustaceans, and amphibians of various types to see if any of them showed signs of telepathic communication. I found nothing credible."

"Does that agree with the Vulcan experience, T'Pol?" Archer asked.

"We are not familiar with any such creatures that have telepathic powers," T'Pol said. "Indeed, the telepaths we are familiar with have powers that are much more generalized—gentler, if you will."

Archer nodded. "The problem we're facing, as I understand it, is a dual one, of both language and communication method. Ensign, in your study of these creatures, have you seen any sign that they spoke once in their distant past? Or maybe still do make any form of verbal communication?"

"No, sir," she said. "They do not."

He was surprise at the swiftness of her answer.

"And you can be sure of this, Ensign?" T'Pol asked.

"Yes, I can," Cutler said.

Archer held up a finger for her to wait a moment, then went over to Hoshi. He tapped her on the shoulder. "I think you should be involved in this conversation."

She looked surprised, but she took her earpiece out and joined them.

"Go ahead, Ensign," Archer said to Cutler. "Explain why you're sure that these aliens never spoke to each other."

Cutler gave Hoshi a nervous glance, then said, "From what I can tell from the scans I've been given, these aliens breathe through a type of gill/lung combination on the sides of their necks. It allows them to function in both atmosphere and water."

"Is this unusual?" Hoshi asked.

"No," Cutler said. "Earth has a number of species who have this ability, and I have heard of many others found on other planets."

Archer glanced at T'Pol, who was nodding.

Cutler went on. "This alien takes in nutrients through a small suction area just under the eyes. To us, that suction area looks like a round mouth. However, from the scans that I have taken, it's clear that this mouth is only hooked up to the digestive track and not to the lung/gill apparatus. In order to speak, at least as we understand speech, sound must move through air. If we don't breathe, we can't talk. It's as simple as that."

"And as complicated," Hoshi said. She was clearly thinking of all the languages she'd learned—and all the ones she was going to learn on this trip.

Archer was beginning to feel discouraged. If the aliens didn't have speech, then perhaps Hoshi's assumption about language was incorrect.

"Are there vestigial remains of a larynx?" T'Pol asked.

"Or something similar to a larynx?" Hoshi added. She seemed excited by the prospect.

"Huh?" Archer asked.

"Your tailbone," T'Pol said, "is the vestigial remains of the tail that your species used to have."

She said that with such disdain that for a moment, Archer wondered if she was comparing him to his tail-bearing ancestors and finding him lacking. Then he smiled. She simply hated explaining things that she believed should be obvious.

"I didn't do the scans myself," Cutler said. "I wasn't allowed near the alien."

"Surely something like a vestigial remains of a larynx would show up on Dr. Phlox's scans," T'Pol said.

Cutler shook her head. "Nothing did. I looked. The structure for any type of vocal cords just isn't there, even morphed through time, and there is no ability to concentrate the air in any fashion. I believe these creatures evolved with no need to speak aloud."

"Language doesn't have to be verbal to be understood," Hoshi said. "American sign is done by gesture alone."

"It is possible that they once communicated like that," Cutler said, "but I doubt it. If they had the telepathic abilities from the beginning, they would develop those, not a complex series of gestures."

"Yet," T'Pol said, "there are dozens of other ways to make oneself understood. They could have clicked their claws together or rubbed their legs like your crickets."

"Sure, they could have." Cutler shrugged. "But they didn't. In those cases, the body parts become instruments. These aren't. Besides, communication like that would be inefficient underwater."

"Good point," Archer said, finally feeling like he could contribute.

"Damn," Hoshi said softly to herself. "I was afraid of that."

Archer frowned at her. She shook her head. T'Pol looked frustrated as well.

"What's the problem with telepathy?" Cutler asked, glancing at Hoshi, then back at Archer.

"Language, Ensign," Archer said. "Language. We were hoping to build a device that would translate our language into psionic energy they could hear."

Cutler nodded, clearly understanding. "But if they

had no language to start with, then such translation would be impossible."

"Correct," T'Pol said. "So I am going to have to be present to speak with the alien telepathically."

Archer had been fighting that idea for the past twelve hours, and he still didn't want her to try it. Even with a device that would reduce the strength of the alien psionic energy, and boost T'Pol's thoughts through psionic energy in return, it was just too dangerous. One misdirected alien thought, and T'Pol might die. Or that thought might make her insane for the rest of her long Vulcan life.

"I'm not ready for that yet," Archer said.

Hoshi bit her lower lip. "Sir, direct mind contact is going to have to be the only way. It is not possible to translate a language that does not exist."

Archer paced down the step to his chair and looked at the planet, which was still on the large screen. He had always assumed that first contact was easy, that the Vulcans had blown it out of proportion and made it into an ordeal. The human-Vulcan first contact was easy compared with this; their bodies, while different, weren't that different, and they communicated through speech.

This was feeling impossible.

It looked like it was time to let this one go, give the information to all the scientists on Vulcan and Earth to study. They had the time. Let them come up with a solution and the next ship past here would deal with the mess he made of this first contact.

But he wasn't ready to give up. He never gave up.

There had to be a way to communicate without sacrificing another member of his crew.

"Sir," Cutler said, breaking into the dark silence of the bridge. "There might be a way."

Archer spun around and stared at the young ensign. She was looking nervous and worried, but clearly determined. Both T'Pol and Ensign Hoshi were watching intently.

"Go ahead," Archer said.

"Well, sir," Cutler said, "you know that Crewman Novakovich has been on light duty since the transporter accident a few weeks ago."

Archer winced. He hated thinking about that moment. At least Novakovich had survived. When Archer had first seen him, the man looked like one of those tree-creatures of English folk literature.

"Novakovich has been, um—" Cutler flushed.

"Playing a game in the mess hall with you and Travis Mayweather and James Anderson," Archer said.

Cutler's eyes widened.

"I keep track of my crew, Ensign," Archer said, amused by her surprise. "You can go on."

"Then you probably know this, sir."

"I'm not sure what you think I know, Ensign."

"Um, well, in the downtime, he decided to make himself useful," she said, clearly uncomfortable. "He had an idea about a shield against the psionic energy. He's been working with Crewman Williams in engineering to see if they could make it work."

Archer stared at her for a moment. His smugness at knowing everything his crew was doing vanished.

He was too astounded by her news to be annoyed that he wasn't being kept informed.

He reached over to the intercom link on his chair. "Crewman Novakovich, Crewman Williams, Chief Engineer Tucker, report to the bridge."

Archer glanced up at T'Pol, but she had already returned to her science station. Her fingers were dancing over her board as she worked calculations. Clearly the idea of shielding from the psionic energy had not crossed her mind either. Sometimes it was the most obvious solutions that were the best.

Archer smiled at Cutler. "Thank you, Ensign. You may have just told us about the key we needed to make this work."

Twenty minutes later, the discussion between Crewman Novakovich, Crewman Williams, Cutler, Trip, T'Pol, and Hoshi was raging, filling the bridge with ideas, arguments, counterarguments, and theories as to what would be the best way to shield humans from the alien psionic energy thought waves.

Archer stood back, his arms crossed, watching as some of the best minds he had ever had the pleasure to be around struggled to solve the same problem. Sometimes he felt very lucky to have surrounded himself on this first mission with such a great crew. This was one of those times.

TWENTY-FIVE

Captain's log.

I have decided that I will talk to the alien first.

T'Pol disagreed. We had to take the argument to the ready room. She was quite strident for a Vulcan. She's worried that my puny mind won't be able to handle an errant alien thought wave. I reminded her that she had said she wouldn't be able to handle one either.

That didn't quiet her for long. She believes that a captain should never risk his life for his crew. The captain, she says, is the most important person on the ship. Crew should be sacrificed before the captain takes a risk.

I wonder what she would have thought about all those old navy captains who went down with their ships while their crews es-

caped. Clearly we have some cultural differences here too.

Although I must admit, Starfleet does suggest that the captain take fewer risks than I do. The entire idea amuses me. This trip is risk enough; whether or not I face an alien who could kill me with a thought isn't going to add much to the risk factor that already exists.

Besides, I'm not going to have my staff do something I'm unwilling to do myself.

That's my justification and I'm sticking to it. Besides, this is an Earth ship and it is up to me to make first contact for Earth.

Once I got T'Pol to stop arguing, she went back to work. She and Hoshi are trying to create a voice/psionic energy translator that will allow me to talk to the alien. Assuming, of course, that the psionic shield Trip and the others were working on actually protects me from the alien's thoughts. Both teams feel they can be ready in five hours.

Five hours. Five hours seems like an eternity when I'm having trouble surviving through seconds.

More waiting. This is something I know I will have to adjust to, but in situations such as this one, it is difficult.

Looks like I'll have to find something besides pacing to fill the time.

THEY HAD MOVED THE ALIEN TO AN ALCOVE OFF A corridor, an enclosed space that kept it isolated and yet allowed a relatively large group of people to work nearby. It had taken Archer a while to determine the best place to deal with the alien. He hadn't wanted to place anyone in danger except himself. That had taken some doing—and a bit of rearranging of equipment—but he believed they had found the right location.

Unfortunately, this tiny area of the ship did not have the same sophisticated environmental controls that sickbay had. Nothing they did could keep the smell down. The alien's stench was so thick here that Archer's eyes were watering. One of the guards that Reed had posted down the corridor was wearing a mask because, Reed said, she was afraid she'd pass out.

The smell—salty rotted oily and fishy mixed into one—was truly another presence in the room. If the aliens decided to stop communicating with telepathy, they could probably communicate with their odor alone.

Only on land, though.

He pressed the back of his hand against his nostrils, but that really didn't help much. The mask would have been a good idea if he weren't trying to communicate. He didn't want his voice muffled or his appearance altered. He wanted everything to go as smoothly as possible.

Trip was making the final adjustments to the psionic energy shield. The shield Trip, Ensign Cutler, Crewmen Williams, and Novakovich had invented seemed rudimentary. They put two pole-shaped machines on either side of the brig. The poles, used in unison, would create a clear energy barrier that would act like an invisible wall between Archer and the alien.

This energy wall couldn't even be felt and wouldn't hurt anyone who walked through it, because it was finely tuned to the psionic-wave frequency the alien used for telepathic communication. When the alien psionic waves passed through the energy, they were scattered and theoretically rendered harmless.

"It should work," Trip had told Archer. "But there's really no way to really test it without waking up our friend."

"So what happens if the psionic energy varies slightly?" Archer had asked.

"The shield won't block it," Trip had said.

"So I have to make sure I don't get the alien to raise his voice at me," Archer had said.

Trip hadn't laughed, which was probably the proper response. Archer felt amused, however. He was living a life he had never imagined he could live, filled daily with incredible risks. This was just one of them.

Dr. Phlox stood just inside the energy barrier, waiting to inject the alien with a stimulant and wake it up. Archer's greatest concern was that the alien wake slowly. He didn't want Phlox to get caught by any alien attempt at communication.

Phlox didn't seem bothered by the odor. He waited calmly, as if standing in a stench worse than ten thousand garbage dumps was normal for him.

Hoshi and T'Pol were working behind a nearby wall. They were putting the finishing touches on their own device. Theoretically, the device would change spoken words into psionic energy that the alien could understand. However, they were fairly certain it would be broadcasting only gibberish at first to the alien, which, T'Pol had said calmly, "Would be a problem."

Sometimes Vulcans were so prone to understatement. Archer had to keep an alien who had been knocked out calm when it woke up, then talk enough gibberish to it so that it would try to communicate back enough for the device to figure out how to translate.

Archer didn't give the entire thing much of a chance of success, but there didn't seem to be any other option short of just packing up and heading to the next star.

He wasn't ready to do that. Not yet. The last thing he wanted was for his first two attempts at first contact to end in failure.

Part of it was pride; part of it was that he didn't want T'Pol to report the failure to Vulcan; but the main part was sheer stubbornness. He was facing a puzzle and he was going to solve it.

To try to speed the communication learning process, Hoshi had hooked up the computer's main translator functions to it. She and T'Pol would be making computer adjustments from a safe distance while Archer tried to speak with the alien.

With a little time and patience on both his part and the alien's part, Hoshi assured him they should be able to develop a translation program that would allow him to communicate with the alien, Archer verbally, the alien telepathically.

Should. If. Maybe. Might. There were just too

many words like that associated with aspects of this idea. Archer liked to have a few more assurances.

"We're ready," Trip said.

"Ensign," Archer said to Hoshi, "how's our translation device?"

She peeked around the corner, even though she had been instructed not to. "I think it's ready."

"How about a stronger vote of confidence than that?" Archer said.

"Well," she said, "I do think it's ready, but we won't know until we've tried it."

Archer resisted the urge to shake his head. He wanted a bit more confidence than that—and to get it, he was going to ask a Vulcan. He could barely believe that either.

"T'Pol, will our device work?"

"It will work," she said from behind the wall. He couldn't see her, but he could imagine her there, standing tall, her face serious. "Whether or not it will work as we want it to is another matter entirely."

So much for the vote of confidence.

"We can call this off," Trip said.

"And do what?" Archer asked. "Have you figured out another way to test these devices?"

"No," Trip said. "Unfortunately, they have to be tested in the field."

"Well, then." Archer centered himself behind the two poles. "Let's begin."

Trip gave him an uncomfortable look. Hoshi slipped behind the wall, as she had been instructed to do. Dr. Phlox frowned just enough to make his elaborate eyebrows angle against his forehead ridges.

No one moved.

"Trip," Archer said, "I believe the first step is yours."

"Right." Trip flipped a switch on the side of one post. Something hummed. The post trembled, flared with light, and then vibrated slightly. After a moment, the other post trembled, flared, and vibrated too.

Archer thought he saw a shimmer between the posts—long and thin, like a heat mirage on a desert road—and then the shimmer vanished.

Trip did a quick check, and then nodded. "Stay centered behind it, and you should be fine."

Trip meant that Archer should remain in the center of the two poles and stand behind them, but telling him to stay centered was good advice for his emotions as well.

"Will do," Archer said. Through the two poles, he could see the still-unconscious alien. It was on its back, its legs flopped to the side. After some deliberation, Phlox had placed it in that position so that it couldn't move quickly should something go wrong.

Archer hoped that these aliens, like turtles, had trouble righting themselves after landing on their backs.

"Okay, Dr. Phlox," Archer said. "I think the next point goes to you."

Phlox ran a scanner over the alien as a final precaution. Archer glanced over his shoulder. He could barely see Reed's guards, rifles in hand, waiting to fire if the alien tried to escape.

Phlox moved his scanner to one hand. With the

other, he injected the alien, then scampered out of the way. "Captain, give it a few minutes to come up. It might be a little groggy at first."

"I hope not too groggy," Archer said. "I need to convince it to stay where it's at."

Phlox made his way beside Archer, still scanning. "The stimulant is working. It will be away shortly."

"All right," Archer said. "Shortly or longly, I think it's time for you to get out of here."

"I could stand beside you and monitor—"

"We had this discussion," Archer said. "No. I need your expertise should something go wrong."

Phlox's oddly colored eyes studied him. Phlox didn't seem confident with this plan at all. "All right," he said. "Good luck."

With that he turned and moved down the hall and around the corner out of sight.

Archer was about to check with T'Pol when the intercom fluttered to life. They had decided to use it to communicate with the hallway, although no one had done so until now.

"The translator device is on and working," T'Pol said through the intercom. "So far no psionic energy readings."

"Thank you," Archer said.

Trip did one more quick check of the shield, gave Archer a thumbs-up, and moved off, leaving Archer alone with the spiderlikc alien.

He squared his shoulders. This was like piloting a test craft. The pilots who believed something could go wrong often triggered that something. Those who had incredible confidence in their own ability and luck usually did fine, even if something did go wrong.

A thousand things could go wrong, but even more could go right. And if this went right, Earth would have its own first contact, a new culture from which to learn, trade, and understand.

Excitement shivered down Archer's spine. He clasped his hands behind his back as T'Pol often did, and waited.

A few of the alien's legs were twitching. It was coming round.

He held his breath. He felt as giddy as a kid.

More twitches. Then something underneath the carapace moved—the eyes? The mouth? He wasn't sure.

"I'd start speaking to it now, Captain," Hoshi said over the intercom.

"Hi," Archer said, not moving or smiling or doing anything that any culture might consider threatening. He had no idea what to say to a groggy, telepathic alien that he had kidnapped.

"Good start, Captain," Hoshi said, "but I think you might need to pretty much talk straight at it for a minute."

Right. He had known that. He had just forgotten that for a moment. All these rules about talking to aliens. With the Fazi, it was don't speak until spoken to. Now it was talk until the creature in front of him could understand.

"My name is Captain Jonathan Archer," he said.

The alien's clawlike feet all touched the ground.

"You're on board our ship *Enterprise*."

The alien remained rigid for a moment.

"I'm sure sorry for bringing you up here."

In a feat that Archer wasn't sure he would ever be able to explain, the alien lifted its carapace off the floor, then flipped itself over, as if it were in a circus, doing acrobatics.

Archer resisted the urge to back away. He kept his voice neutral. "Bringing you here was an accident. It was never meant to happen."

If that thing charged at him now, he was done for. It could get through the energy barrier as easily as he could rip through paper.

"You got caught in our transporter beam."

The alien seemed to be staring first at him, then at the small box where Archer's voice was being turned into psionic waves.

Archer decided to stop rambling and try to really communicate. He pointed at himself. "Human."

The alien's entire body dipped slightly. "Hipon."

The digital voice had an androgynous quality, which seemed to suit the alien, since they still hadn't been able to figure out its gender.

Archer wanted to make certain he understood. He pointed at the alien. "Hipon." Then he pointed at himself. "Human."

"Yes," the machine said.

Archer felt the tension in his shoulders lessen slightly. "I am the captain of this ship," he said, motioning first at himself, then around him.

"Captain," the alien said through the machine. "No need—to go—through—the basics. Your translation device is—functioning. An amazing device, but I—am not sure why—it is needed."

Archer could hear the cheering coming from down the hall and through the com link. With each word the translator seemed to be picking up speed and clearness.

"This is a psionic shield," Archer said, pointing to the posts on either side of him, "designed to block the wavelengths of your thought patterns from my mind."

The alien scuttled closer to it. Archer resisted the urge to move away. The alien appeared to be studying the poles. With one of its front legs, it reached toward the shield, but didn't touch the area in the middle.

A puddle of slime dotted the floor where the alien had been on its back. The stench, though, seemed to be receding. Maybe the smell had a defensive purpose, designed to keep away land-based predators when the alien slept.

When this was all over, Archer would have to ask Cutler about that.

The alien continued to inspect the shield. After a moment, it scuttled backward. It moved amazingly fast for something so tall and bulky.

"Why—is the device—needed?" the alien asked again.

"Because," Archer said, "the energy in your thoughts is dangerous to my kind."

The alien scuttled even farther backward and bumped against the wall. For a moment, Archer wondered if it was hurt. Then it bobbed slightly.

"The crewman—who landed?" the alien asked. "And the other—two?"

The reaction had been shock and concern. Archer felt a pleasant shock of surprise.

"They are alive and recovering," Archer said.

"They were—damaged?"

So he had interpreted the reaction correctly.

"Yes," Archer said. "But they will be all right."

The alien bobbled as if it were still in the water. It didn't speak for a long time, and Archer wondered if he should fill the silence. He still felt somewhat burned for his encounter with the Fazi.

"We had—no wish—to harm," the alien said.

"We know that," Archer said, relieved that the alien had spoken. "Neither did we. I must apologize for taking you from your homeworld. It was not our intent. We were only trying to rescue our crewman."

"It was not our intent—to harm him," the alien said again. It seemed to be quite distressed.

"We understand that," Archer said, thinking that perhaps a different word would make the alien realize that they were not going to retaliate for the harm. "There is no need to apologize."

"We tracked your—ship—as it entered the system," the Hipon said. "We were pleased—when you came—to contact us."

"We were not sure how to," Archer said, not showing he was stunned that they had been tracked coming into this system. Clearly the Hipon were more advanced than they had thought. "It was not until this accident that we began to understand the nature of your form of communication."

"And the danger—of it," the Hipon said.

"Yes, exactly," Archer said.

"Your translation device—is impressive," the Hipon said. "But I must ask—why you came—to this planet?"

"We are from the planet Earth," Archer said. "We are simple explorers, hoping to meet new races and forge friendships."

"With the ability—to create this starship—and this communication device—I would not consider—your race simple."

"Thank you," Archer said.

The alien crossed two of its legs and rubbed them together. Archer braced himself. He wasn't sure what would happen or what the alien was trying to do.

Then it bobbled again.

"Captain—I must do—the proper thing."

"All right," Archer said, not knowing what the proper thing was in this circumstance or even if what was proper for the alien was proper for him.

"Excuse me—please—Captain."

With that the alien seemed to fold up slightly, bringing its legs slightly under its body.

The intercom rattled as it came on. The sound made Archer jump. He hadn't expected it.

"Captain," T'Pol said, "there is a high psionic energy beam being sent from our ship to the surface of the planet."

Archer wished he could see the readings, but he didn't want to move, didn't want to startle the alien in any way. "Are any members of the crew in the way of it?"

"No, sir. It doesn't appear to be having an effect on the crew," T'Pol said.

"What about the ship?" He had visions of the ship itself buckling under the weight of the beam.

"No, sir."

"The shipboard computers?"

"We could run diagnostics, sir, but so far, we've found no problems."

The alien hadn't moved. It seemed oblivious of him, but Archer couldn't really tell. The creature didn't have a humanoid face that he could guess at reading.

"Do you believe we are in any danger from this beam?" Archer asked.

"No," T'Pol said.

"Can you pinpoint where the beam is coming from?" Archer asked, as if he didn't know. He did. It was coming from the only strong psionic source on the ship—the alien in front of him.

"Yes, sir. It is coming from the alcove."

Archer smiled. "Just as I suspected."

He glanced at the motionless alien. So the proper thing had something to do with communication to its planet. He wondered what kind of message the creature was sending.

He hoped he would find out soon. "Continue monitoring and keep me informed if anything else changes."

"Yes, sir," T'Pol said.

The alien remained motionless. Archer wondered if the translation device could be moved so that he could eavesdrop on the conversation.

The intercom thumped again. He would have to have Trip check what was causing that.

"Sir," T'Pol said, "the psionic beam to the surface has stopped."

At that moment the alien unfolded its legs and stood, facing Captain Archer.

"Captain—I have joined with—my people—and they have given me permission—to represent the Hipon race—in opening talks with—humans—please accept—our welcome."

Archer was stunned. He hadn't expected that, but he supposed it made sense. He bowed slightly. "We are honored. Thank you."

Finally, it looked as if a first contact might just work out as he had hoped.

And then the intercom interrupted him a third time.

"Captain," T'Pol said, "a Fazi representative has just gotten in contact with us. Their desire is to set up another meeting."

The Hipon scampered closer to the shield. Archer had to force himself to remain still. He had an instinctual response to get away from giant spiderlike creatures, a response he was going to have to quell if he was going to continue talking with the Hipon.

"You are attempting—to contact—the Fazi as well?" the Hipon asked.

"We are," Archer said.

"Excuse me—Captain," the alien said. "I must—again—communicate—with my people."

Again the alien brought its legs up under it and seemed to just disappear inside itself.

Oh, just great. Now the mention of the Fazi had angered the Hipon, just like a mention of the Hipon had angered the Fazi. What was going on with this planet? Archer turned to the com panel behind him on the wall. "Tell the Fazi that I would be glad to speak with them at a time convenient for their leaders."

"Understood," T'Pol said.

A moment later the alien unfolded its legs and again faced Archer. Archer would have been just as happy if the alien had faced the translator box, but didn't say anything.

"Captain—my people do not believe—that extensive contact—with the Fazi—at this time—would be—appropriate."

"I have a Vulcan officer that believes the same thing," Archer said, both surprised and not surprised. There was clearly something going on between these two races.

"Vulcan?"

"Another race who are friends of Earth," Archer said. "More technologically advanced, however. They tend to not let us forget it."

He wondered what T'Pol thought of that description.

"Understood," the alien said.

Really? Archer wondered. Did the Hipon understand? Or was that just the translator finding an approximation?

He shook off the thought. If he went down that road, he would not be able to continue this discussion.

"Why don't your people want us to contact the Fazi?" Archer asked.

The alien bobbled. Archer wondered if it did that when it communicated with its own kind as well or if that was some kind of polite custom, like a bow or a curtsy.

"Humans—" the Hipon said, "—are more advanced—than the Fazi—as are we."

"I understand that," Archer said.

"We have followed—the Fazi development—for two thousand—of this planet's cycles—and fear—they are not ready—for more advanced knowledge."

"So your people colonized this planet?" Archer asked.

"Yes."

"And the Fazi are native to it?"

"Yes—they had not even—built their first—tool—when we arrived. It took—our scientists—ten cycles—to realize the Fazi—were sentient."

"So you have been watching the Fazi advance and grow as a culture ever since?"

"Yes."

"Did you help them advance?" He was asking this for historical and informational purposes, yes, but he also wanted T'Pol to hear the conversation.

"It was—long a subject—of debate—among our people. We did—nothing at first—then our leaders decided—to elevate them—we soon discovered—contact between our races—is fatal to the Fazi."

"For the same reason it was almost to us," Archer said.

"We understand that—now—with your help."

Now it made sense why the Fazi refused to even mention the Hipon. It would be like living with a cancer that didn't bother you, but you couldn't do anything about. You just wouldn't talk about it. He couldn't imagine growing up in a culture that simply ignored a large hunk of its own planet.

"We have managed—over time—to feed information—slowly to the—Fazi and we feel—that is the best—course of action."

"Sounds like what the Vulcans did to us over the past one hundred of our years," Archer said.

"It would seem—your Vulcans—made the correct—decision."

So much for proving a point to T'Pol. There was no chance Archer was going to accept that idea, but he didn't say anything to the Hipon. No point in getting into an argument on first contact. He had had enough of those with T'Pol.

So, as he had said to T'Pol a number of times, he repeated to the Hipon. "I will take your learned opinion into high consideration. I hope our limited contact with the Fazi will not damage our relations with the Hipon."

"It will not—and we can offer—much information—about the Fazi race."

Archer nodded. "Thank you. I hope my people and your people have many years of exchanging information about many topics."

"As do we—Captain," the Hipon said.

TWENTY-SIX

ARCHER RODE THE LIFT, FEELING BOTH GIDDY AND unsettled by his encounter with the Hipon. He was thrilled that he had been able to communicate with a race that neither the humans nor the Vulcans had spoken to before. He felt like he and the Hipon had reached the beginnings of an understanding.

His crew had enabled it to happen. They'd figured out how the Hipon communicated, why that communication was dangerous to humans, and how to translate the Hipon psionic waves into words that he could understand.

He had the same giddy feeling when he learned he was going to captain the *Enterprise*. The same sense of excitement and challenge, mixed with the knowledge that he couldn't do this alone. And yet, he and his crew were alone. They had discovered the problem on their own and solved it on their own.

They would report to Starfleet, through his logs

and their records, and they would move on to new adventures.

The very thought of those adventures thrilled him too.

But the Hipon's comments about the Fazi had unsettled him. Did all technologically advanced species believe that more primitive species were inferior? Did they all believe that a less advanced culture would take the same technology that had made one culture great and abuse it? Was this the common thread throughout the universe?

If so, he didn't like it much.

The lift door opened to the bridge. He loved its platinum tones, the way the lights made it look like an expensive vehicle, the smoothness with which it ran. His primary crew was on the bridge, making sure this fine vehicle ran in perfect condition.

Hoshi was at her station, resting the side of her head on one hand while she pushed buttons with the other. She looked exhausted, and Archer knew that he should send her to her quarters. She had done great work these past few days. She always did.

Mayweather sat at the helm, keeping the ship on course. He looked tired too, but Archer wagered that had as much to do with the game the entire ship was talking about than the past few days. Except for the trips to the surface, Mayweather really hadn't been involved in all the goings-on.

That would change.

The rest of the crew seemed to be hard at work. No one noticed him standing in the lift door. No one except T'Pol.

She walked toward him, her dark eyes flashing. "The Hipon representative is, of course, correct."

She wasn't even going to wait until he got to the captain's chair. She had done a great job too, but the I-told-you-sos seemed more important to her than ship unity. Archer would have to consult a dictionary. Was a sense of superiority an emotion?

"Let's take it to the ready room," he said, and led the way across the bridge. T'Pol had no choice but to follow.

He didn't much like the idea that the Vulcan policy might be correct. The idea that it had been right to withhold information from Earth for the past one hundred years galled him. His father had died before seeing deep space and his dream come true because of that policy. Now another race besides the Vulcans was advocating he do the same with the Fazi. And that wasn't sitting well with him.

As he passed behind the command chair, he glanced at the big screen. The Fazi planet dominated, as it had for the past several days. At the moment, the southern continent, home of the Hipon, was out of sight.

As if it didn't exist.

Around him the bridge was quiet except for the faint beeps of sensors breaking the cold quiet. His staff leaned toward their stations, trying to be invisible. They'd heard enough arguments between their captain and T'Pol to last the rest of the voyage.

They didn't need to hear another one.

He stepped inside the ready room and waited near the framed artwork. Normally he enjoyed looking at the scenes, but at this moment, he didn't want to be distracted.

As T'Pol stepped inside, he said, "You are on my ship. You will follow my people's protocols. Do you understand that?"

"It is my understanding," T'Pol said as the ready room door hissed shut behind her, "that your people are allowed to freely give their opinions."

"When asked," he said. "They're not supposed to question my decision making in front of the rest of the crew."

"I have heard Engineer Tucker question you."

"Trip knows protocol," Archer said. "He states his opinion at the appropriate time. He is not insubordinate."

T'Pol raised a single eyebrow. "Do you believe that I have been insubordinate?"

"I warned you at the beginning of this voyage about your Vulcan cynicism. You've curtailed that somewhat, but you still insist on acting as if you're supervising us. You are not, Subcommander. I'm in charge of this ship, and I respect your opinion, but in the hierarchy of the *Enterprise* crew, it does not rank above mine."

"Even when I am correct?" she asked.

"Even *if* you are correct," he said.

She studied him for a moment. "That does not allow for the free exchange of opinion."

"Damn right," he snapped. "This is a starship, not a university. I'd thank you to remember that when you're standing on my bridge."

She nodded once. "Is that all, sir?"

"No." He was nearly shouting. He took a deep breath and forced himself to speak softer. "No, it isn't."

She put her hands behind her back and raised her chin.

"You have an opinion that you know will get a reaction out of me, one that my crew doesn't need to see," he said. "This room or any place other than the bridge is the place to express that opinion."

"I see," she said. "Thank you."

She turned and headed for the door.

"You are not dismissed," he said.

She stopped.

"I want to hear that opinion."

She hesitated. "Captain?"

"I'm not silencing you, Subcommander," he said. "I'm making certain you do not undermine my command. Do you understand the difference?"

"You believe when I question you on the bridge, I undermine your command?"

"I believe that you could, yes, and it could encourage my other officers to do the same. In serious situations, that might mean that someone doesn't follow an order they need to follow even if they don't understand it."

"I understand your orders, Captain." T'Pol's voice had a chill. He had offended her again. How he offended someone who claimed to have no emotion he had no idea.

"Do you?" he asked. "Then why are you having trouble with this conversation?"

She turned slowly, first her head, then the rest of

her body. "I believe that our cultures handle intellectual disagreement differently."

"Yes, they do," Archer said, feeling a familiar frustration. "That has been the crux of our problem with the Vulcans since the first moment we met you."

"We are allowed to challenge our commanders," she said.

"So are we," Archer said. "However, on a ship, there's a protocol for it, and you haven't been following it, especially lately. That's all I'm telling you."

For a moment, he thought she was going to disagree with him. Then she inclined her head forward once.

"Now," he said, "what were you planning to tell me about the Hipon."

She seemed to gather herself as if she had put the argument out of her mind and had to remember it before she could speak. "The Hipon representative is correct. You should not interfere any further in Fazi culture."

"Give me a good reason," he said, crossing his arms. "A reason that has nothing to do with Vulcan priorities. Give me a reason that will benefit not just the Hipon, but the Fazi."

"Very well." She hadn't moved away from the door.

Her gaze dropped to his crossed arms—a sign that he wasn't open to her opinions—and he uncrossed them, letting them fall to his side.

"Your contact with the Fazi," she said, "has already altered the course of their future and many of their belief systems."

"I know that," he said. "Since we're already in the lake, why shouldn't we swim across?"

"I beg your pardon?"

"Since we've already made a difference, why not continue?" he said, wishing that Vulcans didn't always take things so literally.

"I am not suggesting that we hold them back," T'Pol said. "However, I agree with the logic of the Hipon. The Fazi should be allowed to move at their own speed."

"And who is to say what their speed is?" Archer demanded. "Not me, I can tell you that. You? Or the Hipon?"

She said nothing.

"No, it is the Fazi who should decide their own pace."

"Introducing new information into their culture will change that culture," T'Pol said.

"Giving them information allows them to make choices in their own development," Archer said. "They already have warp drive. They have made their first forays into space. They'll learn things that they hadn't already known. I don't see the harm in contacting them again."

"Each contact," T'Pol said, "gives them more information. Each piece of information will change the culture—particularly their highly structured, very rigid culture. Your first two contacts with the Fazi did not go well. If the third goes poorly, the Fazi may decide that they do not want to contact other species at all, ever again. You would have affected their development and that effect would be, in my opinion, negative."

Archer took a deep breath. "So, you're saying I should leave them with the negative impression they've gained of humans."

"This is not about humanity," T'Pol said, twisting his own words back at him. "It would do you well to remember that. It is not up to you to interfere with the development of the Fazi people just because you disagreed with what the Vulcan policy was with Earth."

Anger surged through him. Maybe he wanted these meetings in the ready room so that the rest of the crew wouldn't learn how to get under his skin the way she did. She always knew how to make him angry and defensive.

"I will not hold the Fazi back the way your people held Earth back," he said.

"We did not hold you back," T'Pol said. "We allowed you to develop at your own pace."

"Showing an incredible blindness to the way that humans operate," Archer said. "We grasp new information and new concepts and use them. We like new ideas and we like to use them. We are always willing to learn."

"We understand humans and human culture," T'Pol said. "Your people are very reckless in their pursuit of knowledge. I've observed that behavior in you. Your decision to go to Rigel in pursuit of the Klingon could have had disastrous results for this ship. Your unwillingness to wait until Ensign Hoshi had gained a full understanding of Fazi culture before you blustered onto the planet also showed that same recklessness."

"So you Vulcans have only been protecting us from ourselves." He let the full force of his sarcasm out.

"Yes," she said.

He had no response to that. He wanted to slam his fist against the wall, but he didn't. Instead, he took several deep breaths to calm himself. It did no good to fight a Vulcan when you were angry because the Vulcan rarely was.

"We spent some time learning your culture before we decided to trust you with information," T'Pol said. "Your knowledge of the Fazi is a week old. The Hipon, who have known the Fazi for two thousand of this planet's years, believe that too much information will be bad for them."

"You're willing to trust the Hipon?" Archer said. "You know less about them than I know about the Fazi."

"Captain." T'Pol's voice lowered. She sounded almost conciliatory. "I am not advocating that you hold any culture back. I am asking that you not push them forward. There is a third option."

"Giving them the information a bit at a time, like the Hipon have done," he said, shuddering inside. That required a long commitment to the planet, one he was not willing to make.

"I ask you to consider this," she said. "To the Fazi, your arrival is a cataclysmic event."

He raised his head and looked at her.

"They are a very structured people. Their language is so precise that they have only one word for things most cultures have many words for. Their buildings, their roads, their very lives are so rigid that they have trouble with the smallest change. A sentence spoken out of turn is offensive to them, as you learned, Captain."

She had his attention. Grudgingly, but she had it.

"Their only other contact with a race that was not native to their planet resulted in death for their people. That contact with the Hipon probably caused the rigidity of thought that marks the Fazi culture."

"Because they needed to learn control to survive so close to the Hipon," Archer said.

"Precisely," T'Pol said. "To them, your arrival could have been no more shocking had you dropped a bomb in the middle of their capital city. I am certain that their culture is in the same kind of disarray it would be in had you dropped that bomb."

"Because they considered themselves alone in the universe."

"Yes," T'Pol said.

Archer frowned. "But they knew the Hipon weren't native."

"How did they know?" T'Pol said. "They cannot communicate with each other. They know only that the Hipon live on the southern continent and are very, very dangerous."

Archer turned away from her and paced in the small ready room. He couldn't help it. He'd been waiting and standing still through most of this mission, and it was driving him crazy.

"More information," T'Pol said, "will cause more chaos, and we do not know enough about the Fazi to know how they will react to that chaos. I suggest that we leave them in peace and let their relationship with the Hipon continue to develop along its own natural lines."

He glared at her for a moment, then stopped pacing. "I will take that opinion under consideration."

"Please understand, Captain, that with your command comes great responsibility."

"I'm fully aware of that, Subcommander," Archer said. "That was the point I was trying to make to you earlier."

T'Pol ignored his last statement. She went on as if she hadn't heard it. "Sometimes the life or death of entire cultures will depend on your actions. And since your culture does not have the experience of many first contacts behind it, or even a set of rules guiding you in such contacts, I suggest you do not understand the consequences of even the simplest actions now."

"Are you saying humans are too stupid to handle first contacts?"

"No, just uninformed." She took one step toward him, which was, he thought, the closest she could come to pleading with him. "Consider what I have said to you about the Fazi and the impact we have already had upon them. The interactions you have had may seem quite small to you, but I assure you, to the Fazi, they are life-altering."

Her dark gaze met his for a moment. Then she nodded, pivoted, and left the ready room.

He almost stopped her. He hadn't given her permission to leave But he knew there would be no changing T'Pol, just as there was no changing him when his mind was made up.

Archer had been so sure of so many things back

home. Especially sure the Vulcans had been wrong in their treatment of humanity. And he still was.

But now, faced with a similar situation and the responsibility, going slowly and cautiously suddenly made a great deal of sense.

He just didn't like admitting that to anyone. Especially himself.

TWENTY-SEVEN

THIS WAS ONE OF THOSE TIMES WHEN TRAVIS MAY-weather wished he had a higher rank. He wanted to be in on the discussions with the captain about the possible visits to the Hipon cities.

Initially, Ensign Cutler and a few others had received permission to travel to the underwater cities, and meet more of the Hipon. Chief Engineer Tucker, Crewman Williams, and Crewman Novakovich were supposed to alter enough environmental suits for several crew members to travel below the surface. The alterations included the installation of the psionic shield into the suits so that the crew could be around the Hipon without suffering injury.

Then, at the last minute, that plan had changed. Only Mayweather and Reed would be going to the surface, as escorts for their Hipon guests. Mayweather would fly the Hipon back and Reed would be along in case something went awry.

Trip was finishing the adjustments to Mayweather's environmental suit—with Mayweather in it. The engineer wanted to make sure that the shield surrounded Mayweather's face completely, leaving no part of his head unguarded. It was trickier than it sounded.

They stood in engineering, underneath the catwalk. The warp engines throbbed beside them, the sound muffled by Mayweather's helmet. He hated the environmental suit. It was uncomfortable in the best of circumstances—and this wasn't the best of circumstances.

Mayweather squirmed, trying to ease a spot that felt like it would chaff.

"Hold still," Trip said. "You're jumpier than a June bug on hot concrete."

"That's a new one for you," Mayweather said. "You decide to take up reading again?"

"Yeah, like you've been doing heavy lifting," Trip said, "sitting there in the mess playing with make-believe Martians."

"Trust me," Mayweather said, "they are tougher to beat than you might expect."

Trip snorted and continued making adjustments. Mayweather felt the way he had when he was best man at a friend's wedding. The friend had insisted on old-fashioned morning coats, which had to be specially fitted. Mayweather had stood in some San Francisco tailor's fitting room for nearly two hours while the guy fussily poked and marked and pinned everything.

Once Mayweather had asked if he could use a holographic image like other fashion designers, and he got poked with a pin. He still thought that was deliberate.

"Stop moving," Trip said from behind him.

"I'm not," Mayweather lied.

He wanted to ask how long this would take. He was still toying with talking to the captain about seeing those cities.

Mayweather had seen the scans of the cities and the transports that had brought the Hipon to the Fazi homeworld so long ago. They were magnificent. Long, elegant buildings that looked as if they were made of sea coral. To the untrained eye, the buildings seemed to have grown out of the sea bottom.

Cutler had shown him all the various features that proved they were assembled, not grown, and as she did, Mayweather noticed how similar parts of the Hipon cities were to the Martian city she had been describing. He asked her if that was intentional, and she had blinked.

"Of course not," she had said. "We hadn't even known that these existed."

That wasn't entirely true. They had been taking scans of the planet all along. They just hadn't been processing the information.

A bang at the other end of engineering caught his attention. Something clattered behind him, and Trip cursed.

"Don't move," Trip said again as he stood up, the tool he had dropped in his hand.

That kind of command always made Mayweather want to move. But he didn't.

Within a moment, Captain Archer strode into

view. He looked directly at Trip as if Mayweather weren't there at all.

"Are you almost ready?" Archer asked. He sounded grumpier than Mayweather had ever heard him.

"I've got the shuttlepod standing by," Trip said, "and Mayweather here all protected inside his suit."

A bead of sweat ran down Mayweather's cheek. All packed into his suit would have been more accurate. Like a giant sardine.

Archer turned to face Mayweather. "I appreciate you volunteering to take our guest back to the surface."

"I felt partially responsible that he was here, sir," Mayweather said. "It's the least I could do."

Archer nodded. He clearly understood that. "I want you to just drop him off and get back here. I don't want to test that shield too much."

"Aye, sir," Mayweather said. He wasn't thinking of the shield as much as he was thinking about the stink he'd noticed since the alien arrived. If the shield failed while they were flying in—well, they were all dead then. But if the environmental suit's filters failed in that tiny shuttlepod, Mayweather had a hunch he was going to wish he was dead.

"In five minutes," Archer said, "escort our guest to the shuttlepod. The halls should be cleared by that point."

"Yes, sir."

"Too bad we can't take a look around that underwater world of theirs," Trip said. "From what we're picking up on the scans, it must be something."

"Next time," Archer said. His tone was the same as Mayweather's dad's when he wanted to get

Mayweather off his back. In that instance, "next time" usually meant "never."

Still Mayweather was going to ask when they'd get a next time, but Archer was already striding out of the room.

"What's eating at him?" Mayweather asked.

Trip just laughed. "He's just having problems dealing with certain truths from his past."

"What?" Mayweather asked, trying to turn and look at Trip.

Trip yanked him back into position and kept working on the suit. "Stand still. You screw this up and the captain will have both of our heads. And don't worry about him. He'll be just fine."

TWENTY-EIGHT

THE STENCH HAD DECLINED. EITHER THAT OR ARCHER had gotten used to it, a thought he really didn't want to contemplate.

He had returned to the alcove where the Hipon had been since their conversation. Archer felt sorry for the alien; it was on another race's ship and it couldn't even explore for fear of harming the people around it.

In that circumstance, Archer, of course, would be pacing. The alien looked like it hadn't moved.

Archer stepped up to his spot behind the posts that formed the psionic energy screen and nodded to the spiderlike alien in front of him. "I will have someone who is protected from the psionic energy come and escort you to our shuttlepod."

"Thank you—Captain," the alien said.

Archer almost left then. But he didn't. He owed the Hipon an explanation of his upcoming actions. Archer had been thinking about this since his discussion with T'Pol and he had finally come to a decision.

He took a deep breath and forced himself to say words he had never expected to come out of his mouth. "I have considered your request to go slowly in giving information to the Fazi. I will honor that request, even though I will meet with them one more time before we leave."

The alien pulled all of its legs under itself and bowed, or what Archer thought was a bow. "Again Captain—the intelligence—of your race—is clear. I hope for—a long relationship—between our two races."

"So do I," Archer said. He had a hunch humans could learn a lot from the Hipon.

The Hipon rose. "One request—Captain."

"Yes?" Archer said, surprised.

"This device that allows us—to communicate—is fascinating—and would be useful—in our dealings—with the Fazi."

"I will consider your request," Archer said.

"Thank you."

"Until next time."

"Until that moment," the alien said.

Captain's log.

I never expected to have such difficulty with how much to tell a race that is not as advanced as ourselves. I had always thought that full disclosure would be the only policy, that the complete sharing of information was the only way to true friendship. But now, after witnessing the fine balance that exists on this world between the humanoid Fazi and the more advanced Hipon, I am questioning everything.

From what we have learned both from exploring Fazi records and from our Hipon guest, the Hipon have been helping the Fazi develop slowly for more than two thousand Earth years. The reason for the rigid social and language structure of the Fazi seems to stem directly from early disastrous attempts at direct contact between the Fazi and the Hipon.

It had never occurred to the Hipon that their very thoughts were what had caused the damage. By informing them of that simple fact alone, I have altered the future of this planet in ways I can't begin to dream about.

And by coming from space and talking with the Fazi, I have given them dreams of larger worlds. What they do with those dreams is up to them, as it was up to humanity. But for humans, there was never a question we would go outward. For the Fazi I am not so sure. So much of their culture seems to be based on fear and control because of relationships over centuries with an alien race. Why should I expect a different reaction to humans?

In a short time I will be talking with the Fazi for the third time. T'Pol has said that the best I can hope for from the conversation is to do no more damage. I don't agree. I still hope to establish a communication that can be used to grow a friendship between the Fazi and Earth.

I will also continue to work with the Hipon for the same end.

It is amazing that decisions I was so sure of while back on Earth have now become difficult and unclear. We do have a lot to learn, but this particular lesson is a hard one for me.

I still don't want to think that T'Pol is right. I don't believe that humans are reckless. We simply make decisions differently than the Vulcans do. Even though they consider us an inferior race, we have more tools at our disposal. Our heads and our hearts work together and often work quicker than the studied analysis that Vulcans practice.

Because the Vulcans distrust emotion, they perceive us as reckless. But we are not. If I had listened to T'Pol, we might never have discovered the Hipon at all. And our lives would have been poorer for it.

But her thoughtfulness has shown me something too. Her people's experience with other races is extremely valuable. I expected all first contacts to be alike. These two—on the same planet—have been very, very different.

I have a hunch that no first contact will be alike.

T'Pol of course would tell me that I'm only following logic, but I think there's more going *on here than logic. I think the first contacts will differ not only because the aliens we meet will be different, but because we will be different after each new experience. We might have fewer preconceptions—or perhaps we will have more.*

But if we keep our minds and hearts open, we will learn more than we can imagine.

Perhaps this experience has changed me more than it has changed the Fazi. Perhaps they were not the most rigid thinkers at that very first meeting.

Perhaps I was.

TWENTY-NINE

THIS TIME THE SHUTTLEPOD WAS SILENT AS IT CIRCLED over the Fazi main city. Archer leaned over in his seat and looked down.

The patterns still amazed him. The Fazi were so precise. Buildings with the same shapes, roads carved at exact angles, no longer looked mysterious to him.

In some ways, they looked sad, like a fortress built to withstand an enemy that could walk through walls.

On this mission, he had brought Hoshi, Trip, and Reed, just as he had the first time. Mayweather piloted, claiming this was an easier job than flying to the southern continent. Apparently they'd had some trouble with the alien in the shuttlepod. It had trouble finding a way to be comfortable—and when the Hipon got nervous, they did the human equivalent of sweating.

That was where the slime came from and the slime was what stank.

Archer was very glad he hadn't been on that trip.

He was ready for this one, though. He still

couldn't bring himself to include T'Pol on what he considered to be a first contact. Maybe the next first contact that they did at some planet they hadn't discovered yet, he would include her.

The shuttlepod landed in the same spot. This time, there was no discussion of proper landing times and extra circling. The entire crew was aware of the Fazi need for punctuality. Such things no longer had to be discussed.

Nothing had changed on the ground. The patterned walkways still went through large expanses of green, and the plants still grew in the same pattern. The huge brick mall was empty, just as it had been the first time they landed, and this time, Archer was prepared for that.

He even waited inside the shuttlepod with great patience while everyone exited in the order dictated by Fazi protocol. He still couldn't get used to going last, but he understood it a lot better than he had the last time.

Understanding did help a lot. This too he was not going to admit to T'Pol.

As Archer stepped out of the shuttlepod, he took a deep breath. The jasmine scented air no longer surprised him, but that spicy undertone—the one he couldn't identify—still gave him a slight thrill. He was on an alien planet. This was not Earth, and never could be.

His team waited for him, as they had been instructed to do. He led them toward the Fazi High Council building, walking across the bricks with a sense of purpose that he really felt this time.

When he reached the square columns outside the building, the main doors opened as they were programmed to do. He strode inside, noticing that this time his stomach didn't twist the way it had the last time. Part of that was because he knew what to expect, but part of it was because he felt more confident in his ability to deal with the Fazi.

Knowledge was power, dammit. He didn't like it when T'Pol was right.

The great room was just as impressive as it had been the first time, maybe more so because it had dimmed in his memory. The bright light was just as surprising as it had been before, and just as hard for his eyes to adjust to.

There was one surprise, though. The air inside did not smell of jasmine. Instead, the incense burners seemed to be perfuming the air with something like vanilla. It wasn't vanilla, though. There was a peppery bite to the sweet odor, which made it seem less cloying than straight vanilla would have been.

He stopped in the half circle as he had done before. This time, though, his team spread out around him. Hoshi had learned that this was more acceptable behavior to the Fazi. She had also made sure that their suits' translators were programmed with every type of nuance she could find about their language. The only thing she had cautioned him about was making sure he did not speak out of turn.

As if he would forget about that.

As Archer and his team reached their final position, the Fazi council members stood as a unit. Archer's heart stopped for a brief second. Had he offended them again? Were they going to leave, this time without even giving him a chance to speak?

Then the Fazi walked around the end of their high bench and down to the floor where he stood. It was clear it was not a route they had taken often, if ever before.

A new pattern. The hair rose on the back of his neck. They had changed—maybe because of the first contact.

Hoshi touched his arm and whispered, "Say nothing until they speak."

He wanted to remind her to be quiet, but instead he nodded so minutely that he doubted the Fazi had noticed. The Fazi themselves seemed concerned with the precision of their movements. This was new to them, and they had to watch each other instead of staring straight ahead.

Finally, they reached their assigned positions. Councilman Draa, the head of the Fazi council, stood directly in front of Archer. Their eyes met, and for a moment Archer wondered if he was breaching protocol. Then the Fazi leader bowed slightly. "We would like to welcome you and your kind to our planet."

Archer bowed in the same fashion, at the same speed. "It is an honor to be on your wonderful world. I bring greetings from my planet Earth."

They had been through much of this before, but this time it felt right. Apparently they were both going to ignore the previous meetings and pretend this was the first time.

Then Councilman Draa surprised him by saying, "I am sorry for our actions during our first two meetings. We have much to learn about the ways of other cultures."

"As do we," Archer said.

Beside him, Hoshi let out a small sigh of relief. The Fazi council members seemed more relaxed too. Councilman Draa started a long speech on hopes that he had for their two cultures, and Archer focused on it so that he wouldn't miss a detail. He wanted to be able to respond properly when his turn came.

Twenty minutes later, Archer led his people back out of the Fazi High Council chamber, this time with an agreement that Earth and the Fazi would remain in contact and try to learn from each other. He had promised them nothing, given them no new information, and they had asked for nothing. And not once had he mentioned the Hipon. T'Pol would consider the first contact a complete success.

As he stepped into the jasmine-scented air, the giddy feeling returned. This was what he had imagined a first contact to be: quick, simple, and successful. The beginnings of a new relationship that brought out the best in both cultures.

The failures had been worthwhile; they had taught him something. He wasn't sure if he had acquired patience yet, but he did value the research his team had stressed more than he had before.

He wanted to run back to the shuttlepod, to burn off some of this jubilant energy, but he did not. He forced himself to follow Fazi protocol.

After all, protocol, as he had told T'Pol, had its uses. So did pattern, and structure, and control. He didn't want to destroy the structured aspect of Fazi culture. He didn't want to drop a bomb in the middle of this city, to use T'Pol's metaphor.

He just wanted to do right by these people, and he hoped that in turn, they would do right by Earth.

This afternoon's meeting was a great first step.

Archer waited until the shuttlepod was far above the central city and the translator devices were off his clothes before letting out a whoop of joy.

THIRTY

ARCHER HADN'T BEEN ON THE BRIDGE FOR MORE THAN fifteen minutes when T'Pol said, "Captain, I am unclear on the protocol as you described it to me. Is this the point at which I request an audience in your ready room?"

Archer suppressed a smile. He had just conducted the debriefing on his meeting with the Fazi and had turned the discussion to the Hipon's request for the translator devices. Apparently, T'Pol was just about to disagree with something that he'd said.

"I don't know, Subcommander," he said. "Are you planning to say something constructive?"

"I have a criticism."

"Fire," he said.

"I do not know if you will think it will undermine your command."

He shook his head. It was amazing that he could conduct two first contacts with species he had just met when he had trouble communicating with a member of a race he'd known all of his life.

"Subcommander, don't worry about my command. This discussion is free-form. It's the perfect place for an opinion."

"Even one that strongly disagrees with yours?"

"Since I haven't stated mine," he said, "how can you be sure you disagree with me?"

She blinked, surprised at him. He hadn't said his opinion on the topics being discussed. She was making an assumption, which was very unusual for her. Archer had to look away so that she didn't see the twinkle in his eyes.

"Captain," T'Pol said, "I do not believe that we should give the Hipon the translation device."

"Why not?" Hoshi asked. "We put a lot of work into that device, and it can only be used with the Hipon. Why not give it to them? We have no use for it."

"We don't know that," Reed said. "The Hipon are not native to this planet. We might encounter them again."

"Good point," Archer said. He was still watching T'Pol. For once, she looked unsettled. She didn't know where he stood on this issue after all.

"But we have the specs," Hoshi said. "We can always rebuild the device."

"Which is a waste of resources," Trip said. "Even though I agree with you. I think the Hipon would use the device a lot more than we ever will and since we're sending the device's specs to Starfleet, they'll build their own models when they want to open a dialogue with the Hipon."

T'Pol glanced at Archer, who didn't move. He wasn't going to help her in any way on this topic. T'Pol finally turned to answer Hoshi's question, as if no one else had spoken. "Such a device would alter the balance between the two races of this planet."

"So?" Hoshi said. "What's wrong with giving them something to talk with?"

"Because," T'Pol said, "until we came along, the two cultures had no effective method of communicating, and their relationships are based on that."

"Sounds like a bad marriage to me," Trip said.

Archer shook his head and no one on the bridge laughed.

"But, using your crude joke as an example," T'Pol said, "it is still a marriage. We should not interfere."

"The entire Fazi culture seems to have been based on fear of the Hipon," Hoshi said. "I see no harm in giving them a means to calm that fear."

"But to what foreseeable ends?" T'Pol asked. "At the moment the balance between the two cultures is solid and sustainable."

"You believe that one culture living in fear and ignorance of the other is sustainable?" Hoshi asked.

"Yes," T'Pol said. "Until they choose to change it in their own fashion."

"So why not help them?"

"Because it would not be their choice," T'Pol said. "It would be yours."

Hoshi turned white and said nothing.

Archer had to admit that T'Pol had a way of cutting right to the root of every issue. Sometimes in a very painful and deep way.

Archer stared at T'Pol for a moment, and she returned his gaze, calmly and firmly, saying nothing more.

"Trip," Archer said, as he headed for the turbolift, "get a shuttlepod ready, and make sure my suit has the psionic energy protectors installed."

"Yes, sir," Trip said.

"And Hoshi," Archer said, stopping and smiling at his brilliant ensign, "I need you to install the translator in the shuttlepod, and give me a remote mike of some sort to put outside to pick up the Hipon thoughts."

"Inside the shuttlepod, sir?" Hoshi asked. "You're not giving the translator to them?"

"I see no need to," he said.

"What?" Hoshi asked. "You're the one who has been arguing for the sharing of information after a first contact. You're the one who always said the Vulcans never shared enough with us."

Archer nodded, and then turned to T'Pol with an aside. "That was probably a ready room speech," he said softly. "But I'm going to let it go since Hoshi rarely makes a habit of this."

"What?" Hoshi asked.

"I have said all those things," he said to Hoshi, "and I meant them. But we have done everything we can here."

"We can give them the translator."

"Why?" Archer said. "It's designed to help us, not the Fazi. What we've done by inventing this device is show the Hipon that it's possible to communicate with the Fazi without harming them. Since the Hipon have just learned that they caused the Fazi harm, and this knowledge appalls them, they might just decide to build their own version of this translation device."

"But what if they don't?" Hoshi asked.

"Then it's their choice." Archer glanced at T'Pol. She showed no emotion at his decision. He figured that was a good thing, a sign of her approval.

Then he gave her his most impish grin, told his crew to get back to work, and headed for his captain's mess. He could use a full meal before he left on his mission. And maybe a nap.

> *Captain's log.*
>
> *The last meeting with the Hipon went well. They seemed to understand my decision to not hand over the translation device. They asked why, and I said I feared disturbing the balance of the two cultures.*
>
> *The Hipon representative had again commented on the wisdom of humans. I didn't want to disagree, but I sure didn't feel wise. Just relieved that the decision seemed to be the correct one, and that a bungled first contact with the Fazi had led to two different relationships between two new races and Earth.*
>
> *However, after all the discussions with T'Pol, and her pounding the fact that we have no way to predict the impact of our intrusion into this culture, my biggest fear is that the*

next time we pass this way, something will have happened and these two cultures will have destroyed each other.

She is right: There is no way to see the consequences of our actions here today. We can only hope that our desire to make contact with new lives and new civilizations does not cause harm.

I've done what I can. I hope when we come this way again we'll find that the two cultures have come to some sort of benign, peaceful, and happy coexistence.

The last thing I want is the blood of an alien race on my hands.

I must trust both the Hipon and the Fazi to do what is best for them and for each other. I cannot let T'Pol's negative example color my vision, or I will never attempt a first contact again.

And that wouldn't be good. Even though this was difficult, I have enjoyed it—and I think ultimately we'll all benefit from our work here.

At least, I'm going to hope so.

THIRTY-ONE

CUTLER FINISHED THE LAST OF HER COFFEE. THE MESS hall was nearly empty and someone had turned down all of the lights except the one over their traditional table.

The crew was becoming used to the nightly RPG session. Sometimes, at the beginning of her duty shift, her work partners would ask how the game was going.

Mayweather straddled a chair, then rested his head on its back. He looked exhausted. He had flown two missions to the planet and completed a duty shift in the last two days. Apparently flying the Hipon home hadn't been as smooth as Mayweather had hoped.

His environmental suit filter had cut out, leaving him alone with a horrible smell. Even though he had bathed three times since then and a full day had gone buy, he still swore he smelled rotted fish everywhere he went.

Cutler could empathize. She still dreamed of that smell from her short time in the Hipon village. At least it wasn't bad enough in her dreams to prevent her from going to sleep.

"Hey, GM," Anderson said. "The troops are ready."

"You don't plan to die today, do you?" Novakovich asked him.

"I never plan to die," Anderson said. "However, now I'm prepared for it."

"What does Abe say about me in his will?" Mayweather asked. He spoke a little slower than usual, showing his great exhaustion.

"Depends on how heroically you try to save his life," Anderson said.

"Hey," Novakovich said. "Wills are supposed to be written before the adventure starts."

"Abe has a conditional will," Anderson said. "If you're not heroic, you get nothing. If you're slightly heroic, you get something, and if you're really heroic—well, let's hope you don't get to find out."

Cutler smiled.

"I hate it when she smiles like that," Novakovich whispered at Mayweather. "You think she'll smile like that when we actually finish this thing?"

"Are we going to finish it?" Mayweather asked.

"Yeah," Anderson said. "Do these games ever end?"

"I can remember games that went on for years," Cutler said, "back when I was a kid. Depends on how long you want to play, mostly."

"So we may be roaming around this Martian land-scape forever?" Mayweather asked.

"Well, that depends on how good you are, and how fast it takes you to find and retrieve all the pieces of the Universal Translator," Cutler said.

"And we haven't even got one part of it yet," Novakovich said, laughing. "So remind us where we're at."

Cutler glanced at her notes. It felt good to get into the rhythm of the game again. For the next few weeks, her work was going to be extremely focused and difficult. She was going to analyze all the information they had on both new species and see what findings she could make before she sent a final report to Starfleet. She was also thinking about writing a scientific paper on the Hipon.

She needed a diversion, and this was a good one.

"Abe has just joined Unk and Rust in one of the buildings. You're not as close to the center of the city as you'd like, but at the moment, you're nowhere near a sky bridge."

"Thank heavens," Anderson said. "I'm getting so averse to bridges I'm not sure I want to see one in real life."

"I'm sure Cutler can find another way for you to die," Novakovich said.

"Let's not tempt her," Anderson said.

Cutler cleared her throat to get their attention. "You need to know something, gentlemen."

"Uh-oh," Mayweather said. "I'm not sure we're going to like this."

"Coming into your building from all sides are Martians."

"The green kind, with sharp pointy teeth?" Anderson asked.

"Those very ones," Cutler said. "It seems that Abe's trek through the debris down on the street attracted the Martians and showed them where you are."

"Oh, that's just great," Mayweather said. "We wait for you and what does it get us?"

"Trapped," Novakovich said.

"Sorry." Anderson actually looked contrite. "After falling from a few bridges, I was trying to take a safer route."

"I don't think there's much safe anywhere with this planet," Mayweather said. "What are our options?"

"You're going to have to fight in any direction you go," Cutler said. "And in a moment a Martian riding a Martian lizard is going to dive-bomb at you through the window."

"Let's shoot it down," Anderson said.

"Should we be listening to him?" Novakovich asked Mayweather.

"I was going to say the same thing," Mayweather said. "Shoot away, boys."

Cutler grinned, then shook the cup. She dumped the bolts on the towel, and counted the red surfaces. "Well," she said. "You shot that one down. But there are more coming."

"We're going to have to do something," Mayweather said. "Are there sky bridges above us?"

"Two," Cutler said, again checking her notes. "But there are Martians coming down the ramps at you and will be on your level shortly."

"How many?" Novakovich asked.

"Twenty," Cutler said.

"Okay, I see our options as this," Mayweather said. "We can go outside to Martians, we can go across the sky bridge into Martians, we go up into a fight with Martians. Can we just fly out the window somehow?"

"Fly? No," Cutler said, but didn't say anything more. No point in giving them too many hints.

"How about we rope down the side of the building?" Mayweather asked. "Is that possible?"

"Yes," Cutler said. "You have rope, but there is a good chance you would have to fight the dive-bombing Martian lizards before you reached the ground."

There was silence for a moment as the players thought.

"This time that you're wasting is allowing them to gather strength and get closer," Cutler said. She was really beginning to enjoy this. Although she was a bit worried. If she killed all of their characters, would the men revolt? Or would they roll up new ones, as Anderson had?

There was only one way to find out.

"Talk about a situation where there are no options," Mayweather said.

"At least none that we can figure out," Novakovich said.

Anderson glanced at the other two players, then directly at Cutler. "There's one option we haven't thought about," he said, "and considering what this ship has just been through, I'm surprised."

"What's that?" Mayweather asked.

"Talk," Anderson said, smiling at Cutler. "Can we talk with the Martians?"

Cutler laughed. "I thought you were never going to ask."

THIRTY-TWO

ARCHER ALLOWED HIMSELF THE LUXURY OF LEANING back and relaxing in his chair as the main viewscreen showed the stars flashing past in warp. The ship was running smoothly, everyone was back on regular schedules, and they had two days before they reached their next destination. The ship felt calm, a machine working smoothly.

Since they had left the Fazi homeworld, he had thought a lot about what had happened there, and made sure all of these thoughts, both good and bad, were recorded and sent back to Earth. A lot of people smarter than he was would study those logs, take his thoughts into consideration, and train the crew of the next ship and the next.

He liked that. It made the work they were doing out here, the risks they were taking, worthwhile.

T'Pol stepped down beside his chair. "Captain, may I make a suggestion?"

He sat up and turned to face her. "Go ahead."

"I believe it would be in the best interests of the ship and Earth if you considered forming guidelines regarding first contacts."

"I'm sure, given time, there will be some," Archer said.

"But you do not think you need any?" T'Pol asked.

Archer stared at the calm face of the Vulcan. The question had not meant to be insulting. Just pointed. And she had a valid point.

"Actually, no, I don't," Archer said.

She looked at him, clearly puzzled. "May I ask why you think that way?"

"You told me the reason yourself," Archer said.

"I never suggested that you should not have regulations governing first contacts."

"I know that," Archer said, "but you told me why I don't need them now."

She said nothing. Sometimes arguing with a Vulcan just wasn't any fun. They didn't take the bait as they should.

He smiled. "You said I did not have enough information to make informed decisions about first contacts."

"I did say that," T'Pol said. "Yes."

"So, using that same logic," Archer said, "how can I now suddenly have enough knowledge and experience to set what those regulations should be?"

"There are certain levels of guidelines that would apply to every first contact," T'Pol said.

"Not necessarily," Archer said. "If I hadn't mucked up the first two attempts at contact with the Fazi, would we have even known of the level and knowledge of the Hipon?"

"Assuming mistakes will lead to positive results is not a valid answer for any problem."

Archer laughed. T'Pol could be very pointed. It was one of the things he was starting to actually like about her. "I will grant you that. But think about it. We didn't have enough knowledge to even consider the Hipon advanced enough to bother with. Correct?"

"At first scans, that is correct."

"So if your guidelines, however logical they might be, would have stopped us from discovering the Hipon, they would have not served the purpose of this mission."

"Granted," T'Pol said. "But I believe you still need basic rules and procedures."

"I'm not sure I agree," Archer said. "Think about it. If you don't know what you're going to run into, how can you make a rule about it?"

"If we followed that logic to its extreme," she said, "we would make no rules at all. Guidelines, Captain, will help all of us."

"I'm sure they will." Archer leaned back. "And someday we will form them, I am sure. Just not today."

T'Pol nodded and turned to move back to her post. She was getting the hang of arguing with him.

For once, she had followed protocol.

And he hadn't gotten angry. Communication ruled on board the *Enterprise*. Archer was mildly stunned.

He smiled to himself, pleased with his ship, his crew, and their recent work. Then he looked at the screen, at the stars zipping by, and relished all the possibilities that lay ahead.

Look for STAR TREK fiction from Pocket Books

Star Trek®: The Original Series

#52 • *Vectors* • Dean Wesley Smith & Kristine Kathryn Rusch
#53 • *Red Sector* • Diane Carey
#54 • *Quarantine* • John Vornholt
#55 • *Double or Nothing* • Peter David
#56 • *The First Virtue* • Michael Jan Friedman & Christie Golden
#57 • *The Forgotten War* • William R. Forstchen
#58-59 • *Gemworld* • John Vornholt
    #58 • *Gemworld #1*
    #59 • *Gemworld #2*
#60 • *Tooth and Claw* • Doranna Durgin
#61 • *Diplomatic Implausibility* • Keith R.A. DeCandido
#62-63 • *Maximum Warp* • Dave Galanter & Greg Brodeur
    #62 • *Dead Zone*
    #63 • *Forever Dark*

Star Trek: Deep Space Nine®

Warped • K.W. Jeter
Legends of the Ferengi • Ira Steven Behr & Robert Hewitt Wolfe
Novelizations
    Emissary • J.M. Dillard
    The Search • Diane Carey
    The Way of the Warrior • Diane Carey
    Star Trek: Klingon • Dean Wesley Smith & Kristine Kathryn Rusch
    Trials and Tribble-ations • Diane Carey
    Far Beyond the Stars • Steve Barnes
    What You Leave Behind • Diane Carey

#1 • *Emissary* • J.M. Dillard
#2 • *The Siege* • Peter David
#3 • *Bloodletter* • K.W. Jeter
#4 • *The Big Game* • Sandy Schofield
#5 • *Fallen Heroes* • Dafydd ab Hugh
#6 • *Betrayal* • Lois Tilton
#7 • *Warchild* • Esther Friesner
#8 • *Antimatter* • John Vornholt
#9 • *Proud Helios* • Melissa Scott
#10 • *Valhalla* • Nathan Archer
#11 • *Devil in the Sky* • Greg Cox & John Gregory Betancourt
#12 • *The Laertian Gamble* • Robert Sheckley
#13 • *Station Rage* • Diane Carey
#14 • *The Long Night* • Dean Wesley Smith & Kristine Kathryn Rusch
#15 • *Objective: Bajor* • John Peel
#16 • *Invasion! #3: Time's Enemy* • L.A. Graf
#17 • *The Heart of the Warrior* • John Gregory Betancourt
#18 • *Saratoga* • Michael Jan Friedman

Star Trek: Voyager®

#6 • *Cold Fusion* • Keith R.A. Decandido
#7 • *Invincible, Book One* • Keith R.A. Decandido and David Mack
#8 • *Invincible, Book Two* • Keith R.A. Decandido and David Mack
#9 • *The Riddled Post* • Aaron Rosenberg
#10 • *Here There Be Monsters* • Keith R.A. DeCandido
#11 • *Ambush* • Dave Galanter & Greg Brodeur

Star Trek®: Invasion!

#1 • *First Strike* • Diane Carey
#2 • *The Soldiers of Fear* • Dean Wesley Smith & Kristine Kathryn Rusch
#3 • *Time's Enemy* • L.A. Graf
#4 • *The Final Fury* • Dafydd ab Hugh
Invasion! Omnibus • various

Star Trek®: Day of Honor

#1 • *Ancient Blood* • Diane Carey
#2 • *Armageddon Sky* • L.A. Graf
#3 • *Her Klingon Soul* • Michael Jan Friedman
#4 • *Treaty's Law* • Dean Wesley Smith & Kristine Kathryn Rusch
The Television Episode • Michael Jan Friedman
Day of Honor Omnibus • various

Star Trek®: The Captain's Table

#1 • *War Dragons* • L.A. Graf
#2 • *Dujonian's Hoard* • Michael Jan Friedman
#3 • *The Mist* • Dean Wesley Smith & Kristine Kathryn Rusch
#4 • *Fire Ship* • Diane Carey
#5 • *Once Burned* • Peter David
#6 • *Where Sea Meets Sky* • Jerry Oltion
The Captain's Table Omnibus • various

Star Trek®: The Dominion War

#1 • *Behind Enemy Lines* • John Vornholt
#2 • *Call to Arms...* • Diane Carey
#3 • *Tunnel Through the Stars* • John Vornholt
#4 • *...Sacrifice of Angels* • Diane Carey

Star Trek®: Section 31™

Rogue • Andy Mangels & Michael A. Martin
Shadow • Dean Wesley Smith & Kristine Kathryn Rusch
Cloak • S. D. Perry
Abyss • Dean Weddle & Jeffrey Lang

Star Trek®: Gateways

#1 • *One Small Step* • Susan Wright
#2 • *Chainmail* • Diane Carey
#3 • *Doors Into Chaos* • Robert Greenberger
#4 • *Demons of Air and Darkness* • Keith R.A. DeCandido
#5 • *No Man's Land* • Christie Golden
#6 • *Cold Wars* • Peter David
#7 • *What Lay Beyond* • various

Star Trek®: The Badlands

#1 • Susan Wright
#2 • Susan Wright

Star Trek®: Dark Passions

#1 • Susan Wright
#2 • Susan Wright

Star Trek® Omnibus Editions

Invasion! Omnibus • various
Day of Honor Omnibus • various
The Captain's Table Omnibus • various
Star Trek: Odyssey • William Shatner with Judith and Garfield Reeves-Stevens
Millennium Omnibus • Judith and Garfield Reeves-Stevens

Other Star Trek® Fiction

Legends of the Ferengi • Ira Steven Behr & Robert Hewitt Wolfe
Strange New Worlds, vols. I, II, III, and IV • Dean Wesley Smith, ed.
Adventures in Time and Space • Mary P. Taylor
Captain Proton: Defender of the Earth • D.W. "Prof" Smith
New Worlds, New Civilizations • Michael Jan Friedman
The Lives of Dax • Marco Palmieri, ed.
The Klingon Hamlet • Wil'yam Shex'pir
Enterprise Logs • Carol Greenburg, ed.